Praise for Leonce Gaiter'
Heaven: The Rampage of

"The novel's raw, unvarnished portrait of the Old West sounds and feels both grittier and more real than the place frequently seen in Hollywood Westerns and on television."

—Craig Lambert, *Harvard Magazine*

"... not only makes for wonderful reading, but also (surprisingly) serves as a historical case study of the systemic, socio-economic forces that made explosive racial tensions and lawlessness almost inevitable."

—blackrefer.com

"... Wonderful... Gaiter brings life back into the old west."

—Kristi Bernard, BookPleasures.com

"Only once in a great while does a writer come along who defies comparison and compromise—a writer so original he redefines... historical lore. Leonce Gaiter is such a writer..."

—Alvin Romer, African American Literature Book Club

Praise for Leonce Gaiter's *Bourbon Street*

"... New Orleans has long been a streetcar straight to a mystery lover's heart. Now comes a debut book by Leonce Gaiter that deserves a place on that map."

—Dick Adler, *Chicago Tribune*

"Gaiter manages to keep the reader guessing up to the last... a riveting tale of inter-racial hatred and its effects on both blacks and whites."

—John Broussard, *I Love a Mystery*

"It has been a long while since I read a book as complex and gorgeous as *Bourbon Street*... a sheer joy to read from beginning to end."

—*African American Literature Book*

"The ensuing cycle of Mardi Gras violence is set forth in prose by turns as grandiloquent as Faulkner and clipped and stylized to a fare-thee-well."

—*Kirkus Reviews*

"Debut novelist Leonce Gaiter's thick blend of Big Easy decadence, danger, and deceit had me fiendin' for a box of Zatarain's Red Beans & Rice before I could get to the book's shocking conclusion... you'll definitely want to visit the pages of *Bourbon Street*."

—*Essence Magazine*

"Gaiter's incisive prose slashes through these distorted lives, ripping away genteel facades, a monochromatic wasteland soaked in the bright red of spilled blood reduced to a common hue. Purging his characters' embattled emotions, Gaiter lays bare the truth of racial hatred, the years spent in a silent war, the child paying the exorbitant price of his parents' destructive union."

—Luan Gaines, *Curled Up With a Good Book*

in the company of educated men

leonce gaiter

ASTOR
+BLUE
EDITIONS

This is a work of fiction. All characters and events portrayed in this novel are either fictitious or are used fictitiously.

In the Company of Educated Men
Astor + Blue Editions

Published in the United States by:

Astor + Blue Editions,
New York, NY 10036
www.astorandblue.com

Publisher's Cataloging-In-Publication Data

GAITER, LEONCE; IN THE COMPANY OF EDUCATED MEN–1ST ed.

ISBN: 978-1-938231-84-1 (paperback)
ISBN: 978-1-938231-82-7 (ePub)
ISBN: 978-1-938231-83-4 (ePDF)

1. Class Struggles in America—Fiction. 2. Coming of Age—Fiction 3. Road Trip Across America—Fiction 4. Harvard Graduates—Fiction 5. Racial Tension and Race Relations in America—Fiction 6. Cop Chases and Standoffs—Fiction 7. New York, NY—Fiction.

Cover Design: Danielle Fiorella

For JY, as always.

So much happened so quickly that it's impossible to be tidy and neat. My father's death had a lot to do with it, but that wasn't the only reason. The rumblings, the amorphous need for something either childishly simple or universally complex had started before and intensified after. 'This caused that, which caused the other, which precipitated X...' It doesn't work. The question has been, 'How did one barely-a-man wreak such havoc?' This is my attempt to understand. I will probably misrepresent it, but that's unavoidable. The only way we understand anything is to misrepresent it, especially around ourselves and our actions. It's never as neat as we later portray. We take ravaged spider webs, twist them into geometric shapes, and label the outcome a rational narrative. At least then, I'll have something neat to hold onto.

PART I

JUNE, 1980

GRADUATION DAY, HARVARD UNIVERSITY

The beautiful June morning offered a classic picture-postcard vision of the famous university. Like the veins of eternity itself, the deep green ivy clung to the august, columned red brick facades. Sunlight through ancient trees tastefully dappled everything beneath with dancing shadows. I sat in my underwear on a threadbare sofa with springs shooting out of it like weeds, concentrating on the sounds. Six notes. That's all I wanted—to mimic six notes. They had been played with equal parts thoughtless abandon and effortless mastery, mind you, but I sat, biting furiously on my reed and making wretched noises as the sublime 1947 Charlie Parker Dial Records master tape of "Embraceable You" spun on the turntable. I would set the needle down, hear the speakers 'whomp,' set myself on the edge of the sofa, embouchure just right, fingers in position, and try to play along. After note two, I invariably lagged. By note three, I was parodic. About there I'd stop, hop to the turntable, and try it all over again.

After the tenth time, the obligatory "Shut the fuck ups" and "You sucks" faded into ambient noise, easily ignored. I knew they were right, but it didn't matter. Trust me: I didn't sense that I had some grand talent lurking beneath the false notes and wayward time, but I did think this was important. It was a test that I had set for myself. I meant to determine what kind of person I was and what kind of man I might be: an exercise in sheer will. I would impose my will upon this hunk of alto brass and my lack of native ability. But more importantly, I would understand. By playing those six notes as Charlie Parker had, by mimicking a slice of the solo from the Dial "Embraceable You," I would prove that I could, at least from a distance, enter the realm of The Great. I would understand, at least secondhand, what occurred at such enviable altitudes. I desperately wanted to know how men breathed at those all but unreachable heights. Don't look for logic in it. I was young; there was none, and this was a different time—before our media-technological obsessions had rendered moot the very concept of art, much less great art, to most. Back then, I wanted to snuggle up to brilliance, just as today's young want wealth or fame, though I had none of my own. I wanted to understand the oddity of genius—a thing that, like God, stubbornly defies knowing or understanding unless you happen to be a god or a genius—and decided through a quirk of twisted logic that I would do it through the first six notes of the Dial "Embraceable You."

I heard the heavy wooden door slam into the wall as if kicked (which it had been, by my roommate, Paul) followed by a rhythmically endless *thump, thump, thump*.

"Twenty more an' I got a personal best," he said. "Why aren't you dressed?"

He was playing paddleball, a recent obsession. For the past two days, he'd constantly held the small wooden paddle with the red rubber ball dangling limply from a rubber band when he wasn't slapping it up in the air. Eyes to the ceiling, the ball's apogee, he sailed into the room following the ball's inevitable shifts and scurries to ensure that his paddle lay directly beneath it. His black gown flowed after him, and the dangle on his black mortarboard bobbed hysterically with every thump.

"Avoidance technique," I replied. "My parents are coming."

"Mine are here already. Had to go to dinner with 'em last night. They reminded me that they sacrificed their life savings to send me here and I'm obligated to achieve all that they never could because they did not have the advantages that they have so generously afforded me."

I settled the horn near its case and walked calmly through the collision of the room's grandeur (oak walls, six foot fireplace, hardwood floors, Harvard's gifts to the 19th century sons of the rich) and its threadbare Salvation Army castoff furnishings. In my bedroom, next to the packing tape, I found the scissors. I re-entered the living room and froze in the doorway, dangerously snipping the air. Paul dared take his eye off the ball long enough to glance my way. I charged. With a stooped, bent-legged gait, he scurried forward. The rubber ball smacked against the wooden paddle as he rushed this way and that, yanked by the little ball's unpredictability and my pursuit. I leapt on the sofa and sliced the air an inch from his rubber band. He came tragically close to missing the ball, which flew vertically, but with a quick-footed shuffle he made a save as he floated into my bedroom—a fatal move. Trapped. He bobbed and weaved, but he was done; the scissors snapped and the ball flew, disappearing into a pile of dirty clothes.

He fell back on the bed, arms outstretched. "Now I have to figure out what to do with my *life*," he said, as if cause and effect came into play between the lost rubber ball and his existential crisis.

Ignoring him, I returned to the living room and ritually, as always, lovingly, removed the saxophone mouthpiece, wiped it down, cleaned the spit valve and placed the gold horn on its blue velvet padding. I closed the case as if locking a genie back in the bottle, as if securing the concept of possibility itself.

"I said," Paul repeated more loudly, 'Now I have to figure out what to do with my *life*.' Graduation, remember? Liberal arts degree, remember?"

"Get a job," I replied. "Work, retire, and die."

I grabbed my pants. I was about to put them on, but an idiotically irresistible idea beamed into my head. I think I'd hatched it freshman year, probably hoping I'd have grown beyond it in four years. Unable to resist, I took the scissors and cut the legs off the pants just above the knee. I kept the legs bottoms and discarded everything attached to the waistband.

"Of course, you don't have to worry about that," Paul continued. "Dying, I mean. You have a rich daddy."

I was surprised to hear that rich people didn't die, but my family's wealth was a constant source of wonder for the middle-class (just one step above working class) Paul.

"You get a cushy job with Daddy's firm. People like you live for fuckin' ever."

Graduation loomed, and the future—even to the point of its inevitable end—obsessed us.

"I don't want a cushy job with Daddy's firm," I honestly replied. "Shit, look what it's doing to Daddy. I just wanna…" Knowing what I wanted to say, I hesitated at the cliché of it, the childish naiveté. But what the hell. It was graduation day. "I just wanna *live*," I blurted. "Why can't you do that? Just *live*."

"'Cause I gotta pay the rent. You give that livin' thing a shot and tell the rest of us what it's like."

Never a break from Paul. That's one of the things I liked most about him. He never let me forget the difference between me and him, between my wealth and his comparative poverty, my privilege and his necessities.

The instant of sincerity having passed, I grabbed a roll of silver packing tape. I taped the pantleg bottoms to my bare legs. Four spots of tape did the trick. Once I donned the gown, the full length mirror showed a guy wearing pants. I removed my underwear.

"The career counselor said I should go to law school," Paul continued. "When I told him I didn't want to be a lawyer, he made me feel like I was six. My own fault… I made the mistake of telling him I wanted something… and I actually used the word 'more.' I could have smacked the smirk off his face. He said, 'We rarely get what we want,' like he was talking to a child. What's our problem, then? Why the fuck don't we?"

"Lennie! Paul!" a voice from the living room.

Louisa and Eva entered, both sporting caps and gowns. Louisa carried a bottle of Jack Daniels in one hand and a plastic champagne glass in the other.

"Party! Party!" Louisa falsettoed. She was a lovely girl and you could tell she might grow into a truly beautiful woman. Twenty-one and half-drunk, she showed the potential for depth and grace. Eva, on the other hand, was a bit of a toad. A self-congratulatory New Yorker, she consistently "worked the room," any room—it could be the bathroom—literally scurrying from person to person, touching one and then the other in forced camaraderie and for assurance that she had been noticed as she feigned breathless earnestness in all things.

"Isn't it exciting?" she cried. "I can't believe we're actually graduating. Just think. In a few years, Lennie, you'll be the toast of New York literary society."

"I don't write."

"Oh, but you *should.* And I'll be the editor of the *New York Review of Books*... Louisa..."

"Will be married," Louisa interjected as Paul grabbed the bottle from her and swigged, "to a short, balding man with a large income and a mistress he beats."

She sipped the brown juice from her plastic champagne glass.

"Louisa will be in the drunk tank if she doesn't watch it," Paul said.

At that, Louisa cuddled up to him, pursing her lips and caressing his face. "Will you marry me?" she cooed. "You're not short. Your hair's thick and any woman I know could take you."

"Have another," he replied as he filled her glass.

"Do you know who's speaking today?" Eva oozed, not waiting for a response. "Anna Freud."

"Anna Freud's dead," Paul noted.

"So are half the professors on this campus," I began as Paul and Louisa joined in, "AND IT NEVER STOPPED THEM!"

"Oh, Lennie," Sara chirped. "Aren't you excited?"

I faced her and flashed my gown open. She covered her mouth and smothered giggles.

"Oh God. That's so funny. Lennie, you're so funny."

I walked to Paul and Louisa and whispered, "Kill her."

"Guess what," Eva went on. "Daddy said he might send me to Paris for the summer. I love Paris. It's soooo romantic."

From behind her back, Paul madly waved a ball of twine in one hand and a roll of packing tape in the other. I lured Eva with a fake smile as Paul pulled a chair from the desk and set it behind her.

"Have a seat and tell us about it, hon." I slipped her into the chair.

Louisa shoved her fist in her mouth to keep from laughing.

"Well Daddy knows the editor of the *International Herald Tribune*, who's spending the summer on Onassis's yacht. Can you believe it? What are you doing, Paul? Paul!"

Paul threw rope around her chest and wrapped a quick knot. She tried to stand, but I sat on her lap. Paul slid rope around her legs and tied them to the chair. He tossed me a pre-cut piece of tape (I had no idea when he had the time to do that), which I placed on her mouth. Louisa finally removed her own fist from her mouth and guffawed.

"Why didn't we think of that four years ago?" she sighed.

Eva's reduction to an *objet d'art* was so satisfying it was easy to ignore her muffled screams. But then a concussive thud outside grabbed our attention. We went to the window to check it out. We figured they were setting up the microphones in Harvard Yard. Another mic shot a thunderous *whomp*. We stared down at the pre-graduation bustle in the street. Earlier, I had seen the acre of brown folding chairs facing the grand-columned facade of Memorial Church. Atop its endless steps, between its huge Roman columns, sat the bigwigs' chairs, the microphones and dais. Workers bustled with final preparations. The church had given the scene a deathly finality.

Right then, the gowned students and proud parents milling about reminded me that our lives, as we knew them, were ending. I had been told what to do all of my life. Go to school. Get good grades. Go to college. Home, schools, Harvard… all pre-arranged, regimented worlds designed with just enough wiggle room to provide the young an illusory sense of self-determination. These places had taken care of me. The track on which I had traveled had been straight and very narrow. It ended today, and disappeared, leaving a future before me that seemed so vast, so daunting in its unchartedness that it might as well have been a void. 'For the first time,' I almost said aloud, but caught myself, 'I don't know what's going to happen.' For the first time, it was not all neatly mapped out. It scared the shit out of me.

The PA system belched another deep thump. In the Yard beyond the buildings outside my window, the chairs on the lawn between Widener Library and Memorial Church were beginning to fill.

I gazed out the window, wistfully self-pitying, when a face appeared before me. I almost fell backwards as I checked to see if she was floating.

"AACHGG!" Paul gagged on Jack, waving his hands before him as if to shoo away a specter.

We both looked down and saw the flimsy-looking mobile platform supporting her. I marveled at both her dexterity and ambition.

"Hi!" she hollered. "I'm Patsy!"

We stared in rank shock and awe.

"I'm here for the Harvard Booster Club, and we know how much we owe this University, and I'm sure you'll share my feelings that we must give back."

"Cool," Paul exclaimed, ignoring Patsy and clambering over the sill and onto the alarmingly swaying platform. Off-balance, Patsy flailed her arms in furious windmills against the concerted tugs of imbalance and gravity. She did not scream as she fell. I had thought everyone screamed as they fell. Maybe she didn't have time before she smashed into shrubbery below.

"I'm gonna be payin' off loans 'til I'm eighty," Paul mused as he looked down at her.

Patsy twitched as passers-by rushed to her aid. Paul climbed back inside. We abandoned her to her rescue.

"I hope you didn't kill her."

I felt embarrassed at how happy that voice made me. It filled an emotional need, and I hated recognizing those. The mastery of the Dial "Embraceable You," I knew, I just knew, demanded immunity to such petty things. But every inch of me smiled. Very unsure of myself at the dawn of my blank future, I heard the call of a concrete, comforting past to hold onto. I rushed at her. I hugged her hard, and she hugged me back just as fully. Only then did I stand back to take a look at her. And she did not disappoint; she never did. She was stunning in all her paint and armor. Tastefully light on the makeup, just highlighting the glories and masking the few imperfections, she wore a simple, huggy black number that beautifully trod the line between cocktail and after dinner drinks. Her smile acknowledged my appreciation of her art.

"Hello, little brother," she said all full of warmth.

Her eyes darted to the bound girl tied to the chair. Paul jumped in front of Eva, trying, too late, to obscure the view while Louisa hid the bottle behind her back.

"These are my friends," I blurted. "Paul."

Just drunk enough, he bowed, sans irony.

"Louisa."

She hiccupped and over-enunciated in her attempts to sound sober. "We have never met. You must be Lennie's sister. I have heard a lot about you. How do you do?"

"And… that's Eva."

Fury now rimmed Eva's eyes as she gurgled loudly behind her gag and violently shook her chair. Louisa rushed to her and untied the ropes. An embarrassed Paul assisted. They left the gag as they each took an arm and hustled her from the room.

Becca raised an eyebrow, no more, as the two scurried past with the gagged girl between them.

"YOU FUCKERS!" thundered from the hall.

"Never mind," Becca deadpanned. Her eyes burrowed into me, focusing on me every ounce of her attention and demanding all of mine.

"Oh… you look just the same," she said almost sadly, as if prematurely mourning her own youth. "I haven't seen you all year. I wish you looked older, but you're all grown now. All grown."

Not comfortable with talk about me, I shrugged.

"Why not?" I asked. "Why didn't you visit?"

She turned away and pretended not to hear. "How are you?" she asked.

"Fine. You?" I could give trite as good as I got.

"Same old."

"Where're the others?" The plan had been for Becca to meet up with my parents and travel here together.

She fumbled in her purse, pulled out a cigarette, and quickly lit it.

"Mom and Dad can't make it, Lennie," she said, staring out the French windows. At the lack of response, she turned and looked at me. I had nothing to say.

"Dad needed a rest," she went on.

"Is it bad?" I asked.

"Pretty bad."

We never discussed my father's condition, the drinking that had progressed to days in bed with bottles. I immediately wished I hadn't asked.

"... And Mom took off. God knows where."

"She left him alone?"

"She's been dealing with this for years..." Becca said, making excuses, but even she couldn't maintain the pretense. She didn't go on. Her eyes still bored into me, though, gauging my reaction. I resented the pressure I felt to maintain a brave front.

"I thought they'd at least give me the satisfaction, on my graduation day," I said, "of loathing them in person."

"They can't help it," she said. "It all just *happened*. Things *happen*." The last word came with surprising emphasis and she let a scowl of disquiet mar her lovely face. "They don't mean any harm," she said, regaining her stoic smile. "They care about you."

I changed the subject. "I meant to tell you I was sorry about you and Terry." Terry had been her most recent boyfriend.

She made another beeline for her purse. You'd have thought that little bag contained balms for all the world's discomforts. She yanked a compact from it and examined herself as if I'd giggled at a zit.

"The man's a worm," she said.

"I told you that two years ago."

She put away the mirror. "He wore a hairpiece, did you know that? And he still had a mistress from his second marriage. He probably beat her."

Arms outstretched, she suddenly ran toward me and smothered me in a hug.

"You know I love you, don't you?" she whispered in my ear. "My big, little brother. You're so smart and levelheaded. I'm a mess."

She pushed me to arm's length to stare in my eyes again. Her hands vise-gripped my shoulders.

"You listen to me," she said with almost maternal authority.

She stared at me, waiting. Realizing this required a response, I nodded.

"Don't listen to 'em, Lennie," she said. "They don't know anything."

"Who?"

"They. Them, everyone. Only you know what's gonna be right for you. If you chase anything where they tell you to look, you'll never find it."

Her hands slipped from my shoulders. "There," she exhaled. "I feel better." Again she moved to her purse, this time tucking it under her arm. "I've got to go now," she said.

"You're not staying?" I must have gaped. She looked stung.

"Don't be mad at me," she pleaded. "I met someone. A real nice guy. You'd like him. I told him all about you." Every pore in her body screamed guilt, begged forgiveness, and pled weakness as a defense.

"We've got a plane to catch. He's waiting," she begged.

I couldn't speak. It hurt so much that she looked like a stranger to me. Her eyes tried to meet mine, but I stared past her. She moved toward the door. There, she gathered herself to her full height and faced me. She mustered an expansive, beneficent smile.

"You've got wings, brother," she declared with her own combination of sincerity and grandiloquence. "Fly!" She blew me a sad little kiss as if acknowledging the insufficiency of her performance and then she slipped from view.

I had felt alone in the past. I would be alone at a particular moment, or on a particular occasion. A hired stranger would pick me up or take me to where parents should have taken their children. I represented myself at more than one school occasion. I had been disappointed, but I had never felt abandoned—not until today. I was alone—permanently, existentially, whatever you want to call it. An accident of birth, the fault of damaged parents raising damaged children—whether my fault, due to my inability to deserve the love of another human being, or the fault of nothing and no one, I was alone. As Becca said, perhaps it just *happened*.

It changed things. My world shrank around me. I could see out and the world could see in, but a barrier drew up in between. The tape chafed my legs now. The pantless prank seemed puerile and unamusing. I donned real clothes.

Me seated among the sea of black-clad, flat-capped bodies sandwiched between giant neo-classical red brick buildings seemed surreal. Looking left or right I saw young faces which, on the surface, looked like mine, but from whom I felt as distant as an illiterate ape done up in academia's robes. The intermittent *thump, thump, thump* of Paul's replacement paddleball was a comfort—an aspect as absurd as I felt. I smiled when I saw the little ball appear momentarily above the black-topped heads two rows in front of me. I almost didn't go. This was as much for the spectators as it was for the students, and I had none. But, I decided, this was important. I felt I had to acknowledge it—severance, guillotining me from the patterns and comforts I had known. I went late, but I went. Eva glared at me as I took my seat. Paul, sitting next to Louisa, raised his hands in a 'where the hell have you been' gesture.

I listened as students with good grades opined about the gifts that Harvard had given them. Walter Cronkite intoned movingly about the world we would enter and our place in it. I dismissed it all as chatter, like the sock puppet the doctor used to distract you from the needle's prick, as the speaker dispatched us to the world and welcomed us into the company of educated men.

* * *

Post-ceremony tears and partings began. Louisa dragged me around like a rag doll, pitying my abandonment and determined to make up for it. Hugs proliferated and tears proved infectious. I struggled mightily to keep mine back. People ran forward with manic airs and threw their arms around me. It became hard to distinguish one from the other. But the cumulative effect was one of a slow winding down, a clock ticking ever more slowly, warning of the imminence of whatever it counted down to. Louisa's bottle saved us. It kept us light-headed throughout that mercilessly bright afternoon.

As the sun set, crowds thinned while mounds of trunks and boxes grew outside of family wagons. Beneath my dorm room window, Paul's mother stood by a particularly poor specimen. Paul's father sat in the driver's seat, turning the key and triggering a sickly whine.

Paul's mother warned, "Don't flood it, Marvin." Her voice echoed off the buildings.

I heard her husband's inarticulate grumble of a response.

She looked up. "You folks come on down now. Paul?"

He stuck his head out.

"Is that everything?" his mother asked.

"Just about," he replied.

Paul slouched in the remains of our living room with his sullen fourteen-year-old sister, who was decked out in the height of the day's pop star wannabe rags.

"They gonna throw you outta the house now?" she asked.

"Soon enough," he replied.

"What you gonna do?"

"Not think about it."

An angelic string chorus wafted through the open doorway. I recognized it, and so did Paul. We looked at one another, smiled, and rose simultaneously.

"Tell Mom and Dad I'll be right down," Paul said to his sister while straining for the door.

"No rush," the girl muttered, standing. "The car won't start."

* * *

Shadows danced in the hallway like ghosts admonishing us to hush and savor what would come. Louisa had concocted this, her gift—something to help us remember her and the moment. It was so much like her.

We entered her room to a scratchy recording of Dinah Washington selling for all it was worth, a slow blues of the transcendent kind—"This Bitter Earth." At least twenty candles lit the room, highlighting its nineteenth-century elegance, dimming its twentieth-century dinginess, and transforming it into a reverie. The shadows multiplied as Louisa slowly swayed to the music. The lyrics bemoaned the state of man, his bitter, loveless fate, and pleaded to the heavens for meaning amidst the pain.

She twirled toward me, grabbed my hand, and we awkwardly danced.

We loved this song, the lyrics so over the top they skirted comedy, and a voice so knowing it didn't care; it mined heaps of sorrow and pain from them anyway.

"So there you are," Louisa said as my arm slipped around her waist. "Are you deaf? It took you long enough."

Dinah Washington cried how cold this earth could be and how quickly time takes us all.

Louisa looked particularly lovely in the candlelight, foreshadowing the mature beauty she had always promised; silky bronze curls framed a face that made you realize that blush was not a Max Factor invention. This close to her, watching her, smelling her, I knew I should have been more than a little in love with her, and I wondered why I wasn't. She laid her head on my shoulder and though I couldn't see it, I could tell she closed her eyes. Her breath left her in a soft sigh. Of the girls I'd flirted with, dated, or slept with, why did I sidestep the one about whom I cared?

In a final blast of sentiment and hope, Dinah moaned that someone might yet answer her cry for love and make this life less bitter after all.

"We must have a toast," Louisa said, pushing herself from my shoulder as the song sighed to a close. She averted her eyes, but I saw her tears nonetheless as she pulled the needle from the record. At the time, I never would have acknowledged that she loved me just a little, but I must have known. I suppressed an urge to comfort her, to hold her a bit more. I feared the obligation it might imply.

"I thought you'd left already," I said.

"Without saying goodbye? That's ridiculous."

"I almost did it," I confessed.

"But you're an asshole," Paul offered.

"I would not have been surprised," Louisa added, "to see you sneaking past my door with your suitcase in your hand."

She picked up her glass and raised it. "Who does the honors?"

Both looked at me. They always looked to me, and I never asked why.

I thought for a moment. I wanted this one to be good. I thought it should be memorable.

"To friends?" I began questioningly.

Louisa nodded to Paul. "We're touched," she replied.

What the hell? I thought. "And to brilliant futures."

No. Not memorable. But I meant it. And on that last day of my consequenceless youth, I could settle for sincerity.

II

Maybe I thought that after graduation, adulthood would club me on the head and drag me to its cave. I clung to the slim chance that the world would pave me an irresistible path that I could follow as inevitably as marbles down a funnel.

Instead, the subsequent months floated past me. Paul was right. I was that rich. I didn't have to work if I didn't want to. Nonetheless, I considered several careers. I grabbed case law books from the library. Resonant snores rose in minutes. I woke in the New York Public Library with my face resting in a small puddle of drool, luckily my own.

Finance itself was, of course, out. It was too close. I had seen what happened to my father, and I blamed the vocation. I was not one of those rich boys who pretended distaste for money. I knew what it bought and what it could bring. I had no illusions about the level of privilege it afforded me and did not romanticize an ideal of living without it.

I volunteered some, which was well and good, but it didn't prompt the self-congratulatory fuzzies that a lifetime of propaganda had promised. Helping the less fortunate was a fine thing to do, but I felt no better about myself for having done so. Of course, I thought I should have. Thought about that for a week and realized that I simply did not love mankind. I did not hold it in particularly high regard. I had no religion, so I could not regard men as little God replicas and thus unique and immortal. I had read my Kierkegaard and Sartre and held mildly existential views. However, as a code, it offered no more substance or solace than Jesus. Like a mushy cake, I felt undone—strangely unfinished—not a true person. I had nothing to do, no responsibilities, no needs, no dependents, no dependencies. I was barely there, and yet, I had the gall to feel a calling that something substantial awaited me. I just had to find it; doing so would lead to the proverbial home. Some aimless yearning ate at me.

And so, quite regularly, I pulled the golden horn from its velvet bed, turntable at the ready, and continued to chase the Dial, "Embraceable You." It was the best I could do.

The same necessity I lacked had dragged Paul by the neck into an 'executive trainee' position with a gigantic business machines corporation. He had no interest in business machines. He had to make a living.

It seems to rain every day, he wrote. *I am constantly hugging my briefcase close to my chest as I scurry up to a train platform or down into a subway tunnel. A thousand others dressed just like me in middling suits, maybe cups of coffee in hand and sleep still tugging at the corners of their eyes. I'm just one of many. I feel so undifferentiated. I never thought I was anything special, but at least I thought I was distinct. It's like each day I enter an elaborate, unfamiliar laboratory where tubes are stuck into my body and brain, one sucking out what's there, and another replacing it with god-knows-what.*

Inside the place is pure Old Boy network. The walls are done up in faux mahogany with carved crown moldings to suggest better days gone by. Everything's heavy and dark, even the huge pictures of old, pink-cheeked founders and former CEOs that dot the main floor hallway. They're just like the portraits on most of the walls at Harvard. I don't know if that suggests I've landed in exactly the right place or exactly the wrong one.

I sit in a large room with a bunch of other trainees. There had been just desks, but recently, they put up partitioning panels that create cubicles like horse stalls or cattle fattening pens, each with desk, light, and an IBM Selectric typewriter. You expect a hay bale to smack you in the head at any minute. I've considered taking a shit in the corner to see if someone comes to shovel it out.

I guess I've already got a bad rep, so I have to be on extra special good behavior, smile a lot and seem consistently thrilled to run around here delivering mail (yes, executive trainees deliver the executive mail). During an initial orientation, all us trainees sat around the huge wooden table in the main conference room while someone from personnel reminded us how fortunate we were to have been selected from among "the best of the best."

Then a "Sr. Director" (which 'round here is one step below VP and thus requires a mild curtsy vs. the full bow) graced us with a flyby in which he hoped that we would come to think of this place as our "corporate home" as he has.

"If you work hard," he said, "you can be richly rewarded. If you don't," he continued with a dramatic pause, "you'll be out on your ear." A hearty chuckle from all. The girl sitting next took notes: 'Work hard… rewarded,' she wrote.

"Let's face it," he continued, "you will spend most of your waking hours getting here, working here, and leaving here. You have got to have a passion for the work. It has got to merit your best, your loyalty, and the sincere belief that you are serving something greater than yourself. This company had revenues of 23 billion last year. We earned profits of over 3 billion. We are at the top of the Fortune 500. It doesn't get any better than this."

I got a chill as he spoke, and not from excitement. And then he downright scared me. "We are the best," he concluded. "We deserve you—the best and the brightest. And you deserve us."

I deserve this. I deserve no better than this. When I'm delivering mail, I look into the glass-walled offices with the crisply dressed secretaries sitting outside. Inside, men in dark suits pore over papers, stare out of windows, talk on the phone. One sneaks swigs from a desk drawer bottle. They seem so far removed from the lives I've imagined for myself. Grant you, being a kid in the late 60s, early 70s, I had some bohemian fantasies, but I pretty much put the hardcore stuff behind me. I sure as hell don't expect to lead "the revolution." As a matter of fact, I am convinced that you could put us all in bits and shackles and there wouldn't be one. We'd just call it an improved form of liberty. They talk here about how America has gone to pot. They all seem to long for some yesteryear in which everything was peachy keen, but it's like they're imagining a time when they could have been something better than men in dark suits roaming company hallways. But they are slowly convincing me that they are reality and I wonder why we paid through the nose to have our heads filled with fantasies of lives we had practically no chance of living—or I *have no chance of living. I haven't got the money or the raw ingredients to try.*

Louisa, gods love her, had not found a permanent job despite protean efforts. She would call me up and ask endless variations of, "What's wrong with me?" and add, "I feel like I'm dating on a grander scale and facing the same rejection—except by committee."

Now she spent more time than was healthy in her robe and pink slippers, prompting visions of herself as a fifty-year-old cat lady about whom the neighbors sniggered; and to avoid her mother ceaselessly telling her what she was doing wrong, she'd grown bizarrely addicted to *The Bugs Bunny Road Runner Hour.* She wanted to fancy herself a Daffy Duck, imperturbably dauntless, while she feared she was more like Wile E. Coyote, outwitted at every turn by birds. In her present mood, she said, the violence did her good.

"Oh what heights we'll hiiiit/On with the show this is iiit!"

All through Harvard, me, Louisa, and Paul studied great writers and poets, philosophers and musicians—just to experience them, for their own sake. It sounds naïve, particularly today, but we did it… for no reason. We did it… because. Just to feel beauty, to run after it, the kind so sharp it hurts a little, that riffs on love and death and reminds you how grandly ephemeral you are, you and your joys and your piddling little pains. Having immersed ourselves—myself—in all of that nonsense, I wanted to live in accordance with the lofty dreams they'd stuffed my head with. I thought it was no less than my right. This is so important in understanding what happened later. Our well-above-average high schools (public and private) and Harvard had told us that men were what they thought, dreamt, and left behind, the heights that they could try to climb, and not what they earned. I believed that; it was my sin. It didn't matter that Paul was from comparatively humble beginnings, and Louisa from somewhat less humble. You'd be shocked how insular the upper tiers of a first rank public school in a desirable neighborhood could be back then. Paul and Louisa had drunk the Kool-Aid in more public and less rarified surroundings than I, but it was pretty much the same brew. We wanted our highfalutin' versions of living.

III

He had asked for white horses. It was so him—a grand gesture, portentously baroque, but tinged with whimsy. The cement gray sky tainted everything below. Surrounded by it, the white horses shined like beacons. Restless things, they tossed their heads and snorted as if desperate to drag the hearse as fast and far as they could. I wanted them to do it. I longed to see them flying, hooves a blur. Standing next to them and touching them took me away from there. A thousand pounds of strange flesh and heat, they inhabited a world I would have gladly entered. In their world, no one had died. Theirs was not burdened with rituals.

Becca, my mother, and I would ride in the limo behind the horse-drawn hearse. I had wanted to walk beside the horses, but mother forbad it. She thought it unseemly. It was as if this was her day—not my dead father's—her private mourning and not all of ours. Her acquisitive claim made it seem childish and petulant to deny her anything. Her husband had died, not our father.

I keep remembering the horses. I try to think of other things—more important things—but I can't. I stood near them outside the church, close enough to smell them. They smelled like earth—like a link to something missing in me but essential, a smell that made me want to draw it in like a drowning man draws air. I moved closer and touched one's face. He immediately rubbed his head against my hand, but with such force that I soon struggled to stand upright against the thousand-pound beast's itchy onslaught. It left a smudge on my coat. Seeing this, the driver snapped his rein and the horse drew to attention, but it kept an eye on me. I leaned over and breathed in its breath again. The overwhelming smell of dirt and grass and sky almost made me swoon. I forgot that my father was dead. I forgot how he had died. I forgot how he had lived—identical to how I feared living. Despite not having a clue how to ride, I wanted to jump on that horse and gallop to freedom. I knew it could take me there.

Becca called out to me. It was time. I looked back at the small clutch of mourners still gathered outside the church and saw Paul and Louisa. I had spoken to them briefly before the service, but it bolstered me to see them before I ducked into the car.

As I sat, Becca grasped my hand tightly in both of hers. She had been crying all day. She never boohooed or broke down. She just continuously and silently cried. My mother sat immobile. The visible combination of pride, resentment, and possibly relief rendered her still. She rarely moved as she looked out her window. Now and then her eyes caught Becca's or mine. She'd offer a momentary aspect of motherly compassion, gone as quickly as it appeared, as her eyes settled again on the view outside.

It was surreal. It was as if I had watched myself and the proceedings on a screen. The paces were so practiced, the sets so elaborate, the players so well-rehearsed that it couldn't have been anything but fake. The corpse was the only real thing in it. A man was dead. He was gone forever. I had both admired and pitied him, and he had been my father.

I dutifully walked through the process, hitting my marks. I wore a black suit and sat in the front pew of the Catholic church I had never entered before. I watched as an ornately robed priest of some high rank raised and lowered his voice and hands with the studied air of a diva. Before and after the priest, a string ensemble played slow movements from Beethoven's late quartets.

My father was no more religious than I. We had a church service because that was how it was done. It was expected for a man of his rank and station. To my mother, anything less would have suggested a studied rebelliousness, and it was so much simpler and more pleasant to go along, hire the church, and do the expected thing. She would not have tolerated less than the expected because it would have reminded her too much of my father—what she considered his pointless, self-indulgent rebellions.

We climbed from the limousine and walked to the gravesite on wooden planks laid atop damp ground to keep the mourners' shoes dry. We approached the site and the earth's yawning maw open beneath the shiny, silver casket heaped with flowers. The prohibitively expensive box and the equally pricey aromatics were about to be smothered with the shit we kick from our shoes: the essence of irony.

He would have laughed. I loved that part of him, probably because it was so unexpected and like me. A fifty-eight-year-old man who had mastered the look and airs of successful American business is not supposed to whisper wickedisms into his young son's ear, but he did. He shared with me his overly developed sense of the absurd—a sense that never spared him or his own. As he walked me, for the first time, into the new offices of his brokerage house, he had leaned over and said, "Remember *Charlie and the Chocolate Factory*? Well, I'm Monty, but this is my Money Factory!" He had been outrageously amused by what looked to me like typewriters with black screens covered with little letters in green lights. He called them "personal computers."

"I haven't a clue how they work," he said, "and I just bet the farm on 'em. If it's a success, I'll be a visionary. If it fails, your mother will either learn to cook and take a shine to cleaning (which will be easier in the hovel we'll occupy) or she'll divorce us. Probably the latter." I smiled a nine-year-old smile, half understanding what he said.

His ancestry had been one of slow ascendance. Each generation had grown a little bit richer than the last. By the time my father had come around, there was comfort, but not great wealth. His forebears, however, rested peacefully, knowing that the ground had been tilled, the seeds harvested and handed to my father to sow. His own Columbia education, begun before he entered World War II and completed after, had been a family pinnacle, and he, as he used to say, majored in money—the only subject, he had been told, worth studying in a post-war, post-devastated world.

He learned to consider familial expectations his destiny. The war had sealed it. He never left its mindset. The grinding on regardless of anything—blood, bullets, bodies. It's how he approached his life. He did little else for the first twenty years after college than… work. He hated golf and played it, loathed chit-chat and made it. He had the truly romanticized love of nature open to those who've spent little time in it, but he lived in the city and never allowed his rhapsodies to mature into something deeper. He never even bought himself a country cabin. He was like an animal with blinders attached at birth. Later, he noticed the blinders, realized that others didn't wear them, but his world had been so prescribed that some things were simply not open to him anymore. They might as well have not existed. But that didn't prevent him from mourning his lack of access to them.

As far as I remember, he always drank. He got funny when he did. (It was my mother who got mean.) The most exhilarating horseplay, the most hilarious jokes, the most unbearable tickling all occurred when he smelled of the brown liquid. And then, as if exhausted by his revels, he'd collapse in a chair, sometimes drink in hand, and fall asleep.

I was the sole male heir and it was my task to steer the family ship to the next level of affluence. However, unlike his own father, mine was a poor teacher who demonstrated little love for his subject—perhaps because he'd mastered it so well. He spoke glowingly of his forebears and what they had realized, but spoke derisively of his own doings, as if he had broken a chain beautifully forged. His inability to revel in what he had done—the money he had made and the business he had helped to build—it was his great sorrow and failure. He knew that he should have taken a deep satisfaction from it; but he couldn't. As I grew older and his drinks grew deeper, he abandoned all attempts to teach me the lessons he'd absorbed when he was young. He grew more solitary, more taciturn. He went his own way and left me to go mine. That was his supreme failure—his inability to find the zeal to make me love what he so loathed. Again, he blamed himself.

His cirrhotic liver had grown cancerous. He didn't want the news to shadow my college graduation. My mother should have told us anyway, but she never understood why a wealthy, attractive man would drink like he did. She seethed at the vice he had so gloatingly nursed all of his life that it would kill him at fifty-eight, and to punish him, herself, us, and the world, she told no one that he would die from it.

A month after graduation, when it couldn't be avoided anymore, my mother told the truth. I wasn't angry at her lies. I was glad I hadn't known. In fact, I wished I still didn't. I delayed going to see him until the guilt grew overwhelming. I have to give him credit, though. He never asked me to come. He never said a word.

I sat in the waiting room, preparing. My mother had warned that he no longer looked himself. I dreaded seeing a walking cadaver. I focused on the news on the waiting room TV. I remember hearing a commentator opine on the coming elections.

> "And so again," he intoned, "images of rugged Americana, of better days, of courageous frontierism take a front seat as Ronald Reagan retains his big lead in the presidential race. His promise of a return to glory, to 'make America great again' appeals to a country that's seen two decades of upheaval and crisis, but a promise that ignores the more modern question, 'Whose America?'"

I sat thinking that I knew nothing of America. Born here, raised here, I had traveled more widely in Europe than I had in America. I certainly didn't know the country that was going to elect a cowboy actor to be President. I had led a sheltered life, and I had drawn wild assumptions from it. I sincerely believed that you could stop any college-educated individual on any street and have a heady discussion of Proust and Celine, or Beckett and Camus. I thought that my world was a miniature of *the* world—full of folks with the time for meditations on selfhood, great art vs. the merely good, and one's place or lack thereof in the grand, universal scheme of things. I didn't realize that my world was, in its way, as narrowly prescribed as my father's had been. I had been raised to become an Enlightenment man, but had been born at the dawn of the Age of Marketing.

I meditated to the TV's tinny drone until a nurse collected me.

Happily, his appearance wasn't what I had feared. He sat in a wheelchair in pajamas. A robe thrown over his shoulders, he stared out the window of the third floor patient lounge. He looked thin and drawn—ill, yes, but not like he was dying. An IV line dangled into his arm. On hearing my steps, he wheeled himself around and held out his arms. I collapsed into them and buried my head in his neck, enjoying the smell of him again, like when I was a child. I did not cry, but he did. He quickly wiped tears from his face and pointed to a chair.

I stupidly asked, "How are you?"

He cocked his head at the ridiculous question. "Out of time," he laughingly replied, erasing more tears with the back of his hand.

"Why didn't you tell us?"

His smile faded. "The same reason you waited so long to come." He immediately reached out, as if to reassure. "I'm not blaming you. Nothing like that. But it's the same. This is something you want to avoid, deny. I'd like to postpone it indefinitely. It's particularly galling to know that I did it to myself."

"Why?" I asked. I had never asked before, never questioned. I had always let him be.

He looked at me as if deciding if this was something he could discuss with his son, if I were man enough to understand. "I never knew," he said. "I just did it. Or I only half knew. Hell, I walked through most of my adulthood in absentia. I did what I thought I had to do, what I'd been taught to do. I just didn't realize how little of me there was in it, how counter to me it was until there was nothing but darkness without a drink. I guess it boils down to grotesque weakness, so you can score one for you mother: she nailed it. Had I been stronger, I might have allowed myself to see some things that I chose to pretend weren't there."

"You had money. Why didn't you do what you wanted? Why didn't you just do what you *wanted*?" I felt myself growing angry with him and fearing that I was like him. He read it in me.

"I don't know why. It was all I could do to fortify myself with enough bourbon to pretend I wanted more of what I had."

I couldn't look at him right then.

"Don't worry," he added. "You're better than I am. It won't happen to you."

"Does Mom come to see you?"

"Don't be mad at her. I knew what she was when I married her. Hell, I married her because of what she was. She was the perfect wife for the man I was supposed to be."

Seeing the look on my face he grabbed my hand. "It won't happen to you," he repeated, smiling. "You're not me."

"I'm still sitting in my room playing bad saxophone. It *is* happening to me."

"You're young and scared. For good reason. It's easy to follow a convenient path and pretend that you chose it. Luckily for you, I laid a lousy trail. If your grandpa had been around, then you'd have something to worry about."

"I have no more idea of what I want than you do."

"And you're twenty-one, so that's fine. It takes something I never had to make your own path, even if it means… noodling on a saxophone along the way."

That was everything I loved about him, right there.

"You'll look," he said. "That's the difference."

He cringed. Then he gasped and sat up arrow-straight, a stunned look in his wide eyes. "I cut down the meds to see you," he said, gasping. "Go now. Go." He waved his hands at me as he doubled over, clutching for the call button. A nurse ran in and then another as I backed out the door.

Later, I stood enshrouded in a gray haze dotted with headstones and smelling wet dirt as the machinery chunked and whirred to lower my father's corpse into the ground. Mother's impatience emanated like heat from the sealed limousine, but I didn't care. I stayed and watched the coffin disappear.

"I'll leave you my money," he wrote in his last note. "I hope you're spared the rest of me."

IV

After the funeral, the visuals changed dramatically. It had been a bright, lingering summer and a mild September. Then the stage set turned. All of a sudden, cold winds sliced deep. Scarves and coats went flapping and vapor swirled with every breath. Winter came.

My father was dead. Becca had disappeared with her new beau, and my mother had simply disappeared. The world looked and felt completely different, yet I was stuck in the old one. I was waiting for a semester to begin that never would.

When change outpaces you, you ought to be scared, but I sat passive. I just watched the world march past me.

I walked. Every day I took a different route. I'd leave the apartment and head to the Park, or uptown, or to the river. I crossed on the Staten Island Ferry. I rode subways to the end of the line. Old men sat dozing, young professionals scurried with heads buried in collars against sudden gusts of wind, bums huddled for the piss-smelling warmth streaming up from subway grates. The highlights are so mundane they seem pointless, but my actions didn't seem so at the time. It was appropriate to wander, to familiarize myself with this transfigured world. All things considered, I was content in a mobile sort of limbo, like I stood still on a moving walkway through the strange, wintry theme park my world had become.

In mid-October, I wandered to the Hoboken train yard. That's where I found the road I could follow.

The place looked like civilization's toilet—all the city's refuse, detritus, and flotsam had been vomited up there. A soaked, filthy mattress, a pile of old clothing, what looked like an air conditioner's innards, mounds of trash too numerous to count, along with ubiquitous discarded railroad ties, lengths of iron rail, and other transit castoffs. Two dogs sniffed frantically, tracking down a meal. Ground muddy from rain, the train tracks' swerving parallel lines extended endlessly amidst the filth, tugging my eyes into the distance. Even in this dank place, the tracks extending into the void dared you to imagine what lay beyond.

Extending my arms, I balanced on a thin rail. One foot gingerly before the other, I tip-toed along the thin, slippery track. In the distance, three children ran toward a pile of trash. I watched them. In their baggy clothes and pointy hoods, they looked like little gnomes gleefully rushing to check the squirming creature they'd caught in their traps. They kicked any moveable objects in their paths. After three kicks, bored, they'd find something else to maul. With a holler, one leapt atop the remains of the elegant curve of the soundbox of a baby grand piano. The few remaining strings moaned in response to the child's delight. The other two joined in and jumped as if trying to obliterate all traces of it. The lid splintered beneath their feet as they reveled in the destruction. I couldn't resist the thought that they felt such glee because the thing they crushed could have made such beauty.

I put my fingers to my mouth and whistled at them. They looked my way. Don't know why I did it. I wanted to stop them for some reason. I wanted to join them as well. Neither seemed likely, so I turned with arms akimbo and balanced and skipped, quickly this time, along the metal rail. Soon, I heard shouts behind me. I looked back and three sets of arms stretched out east and west as the three little gnomes tottered behind me on the rails. I felt like the pied piper of the damned.

I soon heard another shout and turned to see them soaring off, arms like wings as they zoomed into the distance. That's when it happened. An image, like a waking dream. An idyllic white clapboard house against sunset skies streaked with violent orange. Kids on bikes sailed past. American flagpoles on lawns. Grass and weeds grew wild as far as I could see. On an imagined prairie, a crude wooden cross fashioned from sticks—death, remembrance, and eternal possibilities.

Next day, I took the car and drove south on country roads near I-95. I wanted to see the reality behind my waking dream—lives I'd never led, places never seen. Suburban houses and even the odd picket fence. I found the kids on bicycles zooming down streets. Double cars in every drive. The faces looked different. Less slick, less fashion. I saw less of the blatant striving I was so used to. They looked like they had either found what they were looking for or accepted that they had no other choice. And it struck me, for the first time, at twenty-one, that I was the outlier. The life that I had led was precious and rarified. And if my life's lens had been narrow, then my vision of the world might be as well. I did not know the world.

On admitting that, possibilities exploded all around me. Empty county roads insinuated toughness, nobility, and a people tied up with the land. Vistas shot through with autumn colors chattered about freedom, hopes, and fears. I wanted to see more. I ached to see more horses, wild this time, not harnessed and dragging a dead man's box. I wanted to understand the yesterdays to which my countrymen longed to return. I wanted to know what almost-forgotten essence held such beauty and such romance that they evoked it so compulsively. I would find it, and, if it was worthy, make it my own.

I felt exhilaration—the pounding of my heart, adrenaline jangling through me. A new world presented itself, and I knew I had to tear through it like an unearthed treasure chest: dust off its contents, examine its trove bit by bit. The farther I drove, more and more starred and striped flags sprouted like errant orchids, all garish and loud, beckoning with a come hither siren call and cautioning with their graphical oddity, their elaborate overdone-ness, like the warning implied in a snake's too-vivid markings.

I would go there, I told myself. I would find this America that was mine, and seemed so different from me but maybe it wasn't so different after all—that perhaps held a key to who I wanted to be.

The empty suitcase bounced on the bed. Before I even knew where I was going, I threw some clothes in it, as if to mark a territory, stake a claim. Before it was one-quarter full, I stopped packing, as if attention-challenged, and grabbed a phone book to find the nearest used car lot.

I'd never set foot on a car lot before. Cabs and drivers did most of the ferrying. Our family car was rarely used; I doubt that my father had personally picked it. He probably pointed to a magazine and had his underlings do the rest. With car shopping, I had already entered the realm of new, which thrilled me. I was doing things I'd never done before, tearing down walls of the little life I'd led. I had just conceived an idea and the changes in me had already begun. It whetted my appetite for more.

Paying obligatory homage to Kerouac and the Beats, my heart leapt at the first too-long convertible I saw. Its deep green glowed like virgin moss barely touched by the sun. I wrote a check right there and drove off the lot, already a different person—one who drove a big green two-door Delta 88 that roared like a lion.

My next steps were equally inevitable and each received no more thought than the first. They occurred as if predestined. The phone at my ear, I dialed Paul's house, only to be reminded that he was at work. I looked up the number and dialed main reception. I spoke to three people who didn't know who or where he was before I got Paul on the line.

"Of course you can," I barked at him after my initial insistence met ridicule. "You hate the job. Of course you can leave it."

I never questioned it; Paul belonged. He had to be there. Louisa too. Considering what happened later, I've wondered why I didn't go alone. Why didn't I just point the car and drive? I was lonely, yes. I was one of those people who'd always looked at everything—who'd always looked down at everything—from a distance. I kept most people at arm's length, but this new world I'd half-imagined I thought might offer something more. Maybe I could become part of something and not just observe it from a distance. Paul and Louisa… belonged. They were my only friends. They were written into whatever script I was following, and the narrative coalesced with such ease that I began to think it was all predestined. That's how I thought of it: not the script I had written, but as the script written for me. So with the half-packed suitcase still on my bed and a giant green car parked on the street, I called Paul again.

"I can't just leave. They fire you for that," he said. "Look in on the real world sometime."

"That's what I plan to do," I replied. "I recommend it for you as well."

He laughed. "Go where?"

"Anywhere there's a road," I stated grandly.

"Sounds nice, but I haven't got a dime. My parents are actually making me pay rent. Fucking rent! Do you believe that? It's working, though. It'll get me outta the house. I have to save up for first and last so I can't quit—or get fired for impromptu, premature vacationing."

"Don't worry about the money. That's done. Just come."

He was silent. I could tell he was tempted.

"You're an asshole," he barked as if coming to his senses. "And get off my phone."

He hung up. He would come.

I called Louisa and had a similar conversation, only her objections were strictly pro-forma, like the haloed angel whispering in her ear when we both knew the pitchforked devil held sway.

"I don't even want to hear it," she said when considering her parents' reactions. "I'll sneak away and write a letter when I'm gone."

Eleven p.m. that night, I called Paul again.

"I'm trying to sleep."

"Come with me," I said.

He did not reply.

"I need you to come with me."

"Is this about your Dad?"

"I need you to come with me."

After a silence, the click and the dial tone.

I defiantly dragged my suitcases, backpack, and various bits of camping gear through the dark apartment. I noted the modern paintings of significant value and dubious quality dotting the walls in the half-light. My footsteps echoed on the wooden floors. In the entryway, I grabbed a notepad and scrawled:

Dear Mom,

I have to go now.

Love

Under the street lamps, I slammed the trunk shut. I drove to the nearest bank machine and took out all the cash I could. A checkbook and a credit card would handle the rest.

Then west to New Jersey. I didn't listen to the radio. I was too amped up for that. I wished it weren't so damn cold. I wanted the top down and the wind screaming at me as the streetlights soared like flares overhead and the giant arrows on freeway signs dared me deeper into the darkness.

Louisa's suburban street slept. My car sounded like a slow-moving tornado in all that stillness. Few lights dotted the house windows. I pulled over and cut the engine. Two lights in Louisa's house—one upstairs and one down. Upstairs, a curtain parted, and the window opened. Her hand emerged and waved about. I jumped out of the car and closed the heavy door as if it was glass, making no noise. I heard a thump and saw a lumpish backpack lying on the ground beneath the window. Then a suitcase fell. The house was spitting luggage. I bent low and ran toward the baggage. I don't know why, but I crouched as if snipers lined the rooftops. I grabbed the backpack and the suitcase and ran back to the car, popped the trunk and threw them in. I turned to see yet another bag fly—a green garbage bag this time. As I ran back to fetch it, another one hit me on the head.

"What the fuck are you doing?" I muttered as if she could hear me. I looked up and her head popped out the window. "You bringin' furniture, too?" I whispered. She covered her mouth, giggled, and disappeared as another bag fell next to me. Bags in each hand, I scurried back to the car, where I turned and saw her head emerge once more as a fire-preparedness rope ladder clattered, its wooden footing knocking like maracas. It was so loud in the quiet that I ducked and covered as if lumber had come crashing down. I could have killed her. She then parked her butt on the sill, slipped her foot onto the first rung, and climbed down. I quietly shut the trunk and walked to the driver's side, but I saw her edging along the side of the house toward the lighted first floor window. Again, I could have killed her. In my WWI trench crouch, I hustled toward her as she peered into the lighted kitchen. I grabbed her shirt and tugged, but she shook me off. I looked inside. Her parents sat at the kitchen table, some papers, maybe bills, lying in front of them. Her father's forehead rested on his hand in a gesture that reeked of exhaustion. Her mother sipped coffee, regarding him with mild disgust. Louisa avoided my questioning gaze as she turned and walked toward the car.

We didn't speak. Only the car's grumble and the tires' buzz. I looked at her, but I couldn't tell what she was thinking. Remorse? Perhaps guilt for adding to the sorrowful tableau we'd glimpsed in her kitchen? Of course she felt my stare, but she ignored it. I let her be. This whole process—the packing, the driving, and the roads laid out before us… the past ripped free from the future; fission occurred; wreckage followed. But I sensed in my soul that it would be worth it. The future seemed palpable, like I could reach into the night, extend my hand along the white center line and grab it, examine it like a snow globe, shake it up and see what happened. It knotted my stomach. I shot through darkness at 70 mph, not knowing what I'd be borne into on the other side, except that it would be extraordinary. We sat in our green eight-cylinder escape pod, intensely aware of the savagery with which we had severed our ties, reveling in and terrified of how unmoored we felt.

* * *

The sky lightened.

"Where are we going?" Louisa finally asked.

"To get Paul," I said.

As we hit the city, metal shutters clanked open as shop workers hosed down sidewalks. We stopped at a breakfast joint and took a booth.

"Why didn't you pick him up first?" Louisa asked. "He lives closer to you."

"He said, 'No.'" I replied.

Her coffee cup paused. "Then why, pray tell, are we going to get him?"

"Because he's coming."

The cup smacked back down on the table. I started excusing my hubris before she could even speak.

"He hates that job. He's as lost as you or me and you know it."

"For him to decide," she sing-songed.

"And he will," I sing-songed back.

"What are you gonna do, kidnap him?"

"If necessary. But I don't think it'll come to that."

After downing enough coffee to counter the lack of sleep, we headed downtown.

It was pushing 8 a.m. The world, our world, the one we planned to flee, chugged to life. People multiplied on the streets. Stragglers became crowds. Ditto the cars. We sat on a marble border outside Paul's office. Louisa watched women scurry by in dress coats and sneakers.

"I should be one of those," she said. I couldn't tell if she was envious, mournful, or relieved.

The ground spat humans as if it hated the taste of them. The noise propagated and dispersed until it reached a steady hum punctuated by car screeches, honks, and tire squeals. We turned to each other and smiled. It was clear we were thinking the same thing: that we sat like visitors from another world come to view the peculiar habits of aliens. We hovered, our feet not quite touching the ground, and it was wonderful. Perhaps a gust of wind would push us somewhere, or we'd flap our arms and head 'thataway.' It didn't matter.

"Perhaps they can't even see us."

I had plunged so deep into the daydream that for a millisecond I swore I heard her thoughts and not her voice. But to test the theory of ourselves as sprites, I extended my dangling leg. A passerby dodged it, to my momentary disappointment.

"I can't believe we're doing this," Louisa said, giggling guiltily.

I spotted Paul walking toward us, his soft leather briefcase—a graduation gift—tucked under his arm. He lit up with surprise. We slid from our perch.

"What are you doing here?" he gaped.

"We're coming to take you away," Louisa leered.

"C'mon Paul," I said.

He looked at us, disbelieving. "Is this still about your little trip?"

"It's happening," I replied. I waved toward the car.

"That's yours?"

"Yep."

"They run outta buses?"

"You love it."

"How did he sucker you in?" he asked Louisa.

"I," she said, "have nothing to lose."

"I," he countered, "have a job." And at that he raised his hand to wave goodbye as he backed through the glass doors. "But I do envy you," he called.

Louisa shrugged as if defeated.

"Wait here," I told her and entered the Associated Business Machines building.

I strode past the guard station where a woman stood signing in as if I not only belonged, but owned the joint, not deigning to make eye contact with the uniformed guard as he glanced my way. Appearing to have so vital and virtuous a mission, I was not questioned. The guard turned his attention back to the female guest signing the logbook. I couldn't stop as I walked past the directory; that would have unmasked my 'I know where I'm going' feint, so on the move I hurriedly scanned the directory for the most likely floor. It wasn't Accounting, not Customer Service; I was running out of time and couldn't walk any slower when I found Human Resources on ten so I slid into an open elevator and headed there.

The elevator disgorged me in front of a reception desk, which I approached to face a large perm with a pair of shoulder pads beneath it.

"Hi, there," I said with a smile, placing my hands on the ledge before her to suggest ease and trustworthiness. She smiled politely.

"What can I do for you?" she asked.

"I'm looking for Paul Gerard," I said.

"What department is he in?" she asked, turning to her laminated list.

"I'm not sure. He's an executive trainee."

"That would be the mailroom," she said.

My knees almost buckled. "The mailroom?" I asked, incredulous. Then I remembered Paul had mentioned that in his letter. He had to deliver executive mail.

"That's how they start the day," she added. "He'll be out and about now, hard to say where. Can I leave him a message?"

"I'm afraid it's very important," I lied. "I have some news I thought I should deliver in person."

"Oh, I hope everything's all right." Her concern seemed so sincere that I felt guilty about lying to her.

"I was at school with him," I continued, desperately trying to make something up, "and there was news about one of our classmates. A good friend. She's ill, very ill, and in the hospital here in town and I knew he'd want to know."

"Aaahh, I'm so sorry," she said, her open palm to her chest. I felt awful, but in for a penny…

She glanced at her clock and referenced her laminated sheets again. "You might find him on six," she said. "They rotate, but it looks like he's got production this week."

"Thank you," I said. *Bless you,* I thought, as I turned for the elevator.

On six, I faced an empty reception desk and scooted immediately to peer down the hallway on the right. I saw dark suits and secretaries, but no Paul. The layout was U-shaped so I jogged to the left, and there he was, standing next to a little black cart with rubber-banded stacks of mail on it. He placed some on a secretary's desk and pushed his cart to the next.

The décor was slightly different. The walls between the secretaries and their bosses were glass here, but it reminded me of the office to which my father took me as a child. His office. Where he made the money that bought the dream that built the house that pleased the wife that furnished the life that made him drink himself to death. They all looked busy, the secretaries either on the phone or typing away or scooting in and out of bosses' offices. The suited men walked assuredly about, looking at home and in charge of not only themselves, but of everything. They angered me. Their swagger and self-satisfaction. On the phone in his office, one of them waved frantically at his secretary through the glass and when he caught her eye, used his hand to mimic drinking something in a signal for her to offer libation. Two of them talking in the hallway suddenly threw their heads back and guffawed, one slapping the other's shoulder in privileged camaraderie. I saw their very existence as a challenge and chastisement—that I should have walked among them, that it was my duty and birthright to do so. That this vaporous 'more' I sought was child's make-believe pyrrhically challenging what every fool knew to be the proper order of things—a brotherhood of confident men in suits ruling the world through commerce. But their gold was my tin. I knew; I felt in my bones that there was a world infinitely richer than the one inside that building, and actions more worth the doing and lives more worth living. I felt it with a literal vengeance. I was going to show them all, all these men who didn't know who I was, but who, to my mind, presumed fealty and fraternity. I was giddy with determination that they would have neither from me.

I glided over to Paul and tapped him on the shoulder. He scowled and looked from side to side hoping no one had noticed.

"Are you nuts?" he whispered. "What the fuck are you doing here?"

"Come with us," I said… demanded… pleaded.

"Jesus," he rolled his eyes. He pushed the cart to the next desk and grabbed a bundle of mail. "Get outta here before you get me fired," he said, glancing at me long enough to show his embarrassment. He put mail on a secretary's desk. He might as well have been delivering sandwiches.

"This isn't mine," she tsked, annoyed, and tossed the mail back at the cart. Half of it fell on the floor, a fact she ignored. Paul's face turned beet red as he bent to pick up the mess on the floor. He and I had sat, rapt, watching Pierrot le Fou unfold like a technicolor fever dream; staring at Vermeer's *Girl with a Red Hat*, we had reordered the world along principles of shadow and light; we had stared down sunsets with cosmology texts in hand and done our damnedest to project ourselves to the end of time. Now, for a living, he picked up interoffice memos that someone had thrown at his feet.

"Pardon me, ma'am," I said, picking another bundle from the cart. "Are you Andrew Henderson?"

"Me? No!"

"Oh… sorry." I dropped that bundle on her desk and pulled another.

"Howard S.?"

"Of course not." I dropped that one on her desk and took another. "Get that off my desk," she barked.

"You must be William Erlington!" I enthused, dumping another mail load on her laden desk.

She stood and frantically snatched the mail up from her desk as if leaving it a moment longer would cause it to root. "You stop this," she insisted, still snatching.

Paul had stood there, baffled, as if he'd wandered into a performance art piece and didn't quite know what to make of it.

"Then who are you?" I asked, "aside from a nasty piece of work beneath a bad perm?"

"I'm calling security," she proclaimed, lunging for the phone.

Paul woke from his trance. "Lennie," he said, putting a hand on my arm.

I pulled the next bundle. "Allan McCaffrey," I shouted at the top of my lungs, waving the mail over my head. "Allan McCaffrey."

A confused woman raised her hand.

"Heads up!" I chucked the banded bundle 30 feet to her. She rose and caught it, erupting in a surprised, delighted smile at having done so.

"Patrick G. Do I have a Patrick G?" I shouted.

Another secretary rose and took the pass. She missed, eliciting sympathetic "aahs" from some while others shook their heads in outrage.

I picked up another bundle, and this one I handed to Paul.

He paused a moment, looked at the bundle and then at me, and finally grasped it firmly with both hands.

"Okay, girls," he roared. "Victoria… this one's for you," and he let it sail to the end of the hall. Victoria rose from her seat and dove to the aisle like a wide receiver, reached out her hand and snatched that package, tucking it professionally to her chest and raising her hands in triumph. Applause erupted and security poured out of the elevator.

"I think it's time to go," Paul said. "It's been fun, kids," Paul announced. "Luv ya!" and darted to the emergency exit, me hot on his heels.

We dove down six flights of steps, charged through the lobby, and landed on the street. Louisa stood outside the car, waiting.

"Get in the car! Get in the car! Go! Go!" we both shouted at her.

She froze until she saw two uniformed security guards running after us. She opened the door. "Shit!" she yelled. "I don't have the keys."

I yanked the keys from my pocket and threw them at her. With a brilliant catch, she unlocked the doors and climbed behind the wheel. Paul jerked the passenger door and dove onto the capacious seat and I jumped right on top of him. The door slammed as Louisa tore out, adding to the chaos of tire squeals and horns.

"What the hell happened?" she cried.

I started laughing. Paul, breathing heavily, brow furrowed, also broke a smile, which infuriated him, so he leaned back and kicked me. He liked it so well that he used both feet. I was reduced to hysterics. I couldn't breathe I was laughing so hard. Soon Paul, too, succumbed.

"What the hell happened?" Louisa demanded. Neither of us could talk. I waved my arm around, begging her patience, until I stopped choking. Paul landed a final kick.

"He got my ass fired!"

"You helped," I blurted between coughs.

Another fit of laughter.

"What happened!" Louisa yelled.

Paul explained.

"I cyaaan't. I cyaaan't," I mocked his earlier protestations, eliciting another kick.

"I couldn't!"

"You did."

There was power in that. It silenced us. To have *done* something, something unexpected, to have freed a part of ourselves that we'd half-hoped and half-feared existed—it fortified us. It said that we might become more than we had been. I interpreted Paul's look as acknowledgment of that. Not a 'thank you,' but acknowledgment. He acknowledged that what he had considered unthinkable was, in fact, possible. It had happened. Yes: he acknowledged that something had changed, and in doing so, he accepted the daunting, exhilarating concept of endless possibility. Awe of it overwhelmed everything else.

"You may have to completely rewrite yourself after this," I told him. He looked at me with a mixture of pique and injured pride.

"I'm good as I am," he said.

We drove to his house. "My mother's still home," he said, noting her car in the driveway. "It's her late day."

Louisa and I waited in the car. Soon we heard shouting. After a few minutes, the front door opened. Paul emerged, lugging a duffel bag. As he tried to shut the door, his mother yanked it wide and marched after him wearing a businesslike blue skirt suit and white blouse. She grabbed the bag. I heard her say, "You're not going anywhere! Not until we discuss this with your father."

"It has nothing to do with you, or him," Paul replied, continuing to the car. His mother then grabbed the duffel handle and tried to snatch the bag from him. He yanked back. They stopped a moment and looked at one another, and then each pulled with all of his or her might. It was a game of tug-of-war with a duffel bag.

When Paul had snatched the bag from her, he responded to her look of surprise with one of sympathy and resolve.

"I'll call you," he said as he backed toward the car. "I love you," he said, still backing away. "You wanted me outta here and you know it." He smiled, and she did not. As we drove away, I saw her, a living exclamation point of shock and sadness, in the rearview mirror. Another severance.

V

What relief we felt as we abandoned the freeway for side roads along Route 81. Open spaces barely dotted with homes that smacked of the unspoiled world I'd imagined. I wondered what went on there, what wholesome, honorable thoughts occupied local minds, because in a place like this, I knew, only honorable thoughts would occur. I had no idea what comprised honorable thoughts, but I knew they came from people not like me. It was those people I sought. I wanted them to be all that I had envisioned, what the pundits and politicians claimed—full of honesty and righteousness born of—born of what? But I knew the honor and uprightness were supposed to be there, if only by virtue of them being good, plain American folk, something that my pedigree and money said that I could never be. Sometimes, out of the windows of the car, I thought I saw it—or, more accurately, places I imagined rife with it. But then a sad little town would intervene, looking half dead, the paint and gutters, the very skin peeling off of it, its inhabitants like prisoners. I'd pin my eyes to the line in the road and drive a little faster, fleeing the blight on my noble vision.

Paul and I argued. He kept seeing a tawdry "Tobacco Road," where I was desperate for Steinbeckian splendor. He whispered, "Suuuuwee!" in my ear as we entered a rustic Virginia diner.

Stringy hair badly cut, teeth missing, and prematurely lined skin reeked of trips through life the hard way. I tried not to glorify them, not to James Agee and Dorothea Lange them. And I tried not to pity them either, but it was hard. They inhabited such a different world from mine that empathy—the only escape hatch from pity and glorification—empathy was out of the question. I wanted something from them; I wanted a glimpse of what I considered their unimaginably rich souls. Pity and glorification were the price to pay for getting it.

"What do you think?" Paul asked. "That anyone in bad clothes is the salt o' the earth? That someone's somehow better because they read *People Magazine* instead of *Harper's*?"

"I don't dismiss them."

"Get off your high horse. It was a joke. *Deliverance*, Get it?"

"Can't you admit that there might be something more honest here?"

"No. I can't. Because it's bullshit." He looked around the diner. "And if this is honest, give me lies padded with lots and lots of cash. I'm sure they'd take it, too."

We both looked at Louisa, who had a burger to her lips. She took a quick bite and dropped the messy burger. She wiggled her fingers to loosen the greasy leavings as she grabbed a paper napkin.

"I think you're both assholes," she offered as she leaned toward the straw standing in her milkshake. She slurped loudly. "I want to stop in that thrift store down the street before we go."

Louisa hunted treasures. She'd filled the floor of the back seat with bags of dresses that looked like grandma's castoffs, shoes that had danced the foxtrot sans irony, veiled funereal hats, not to mention throws, wraps, and even a cape or two. She exhausted her own funds quite early and then regularly threw items at me with a tossed off "must have," as she continued browsing.

We noticed the other people in the stores, sometimes the shop owners themselves, staring at us. We made a point of not making too much noise, to smother our condescending giddiness at seeing a last decade's tacky lamp marked "antique." We tiptoed and whispered. We didn't belong. It didn't seem right to intrude, as if this world were made of glass that we didn't dare break, as if our presence would shatter this American fragility. Paul too often wore a Harvard T-shirt, which only made things worse.

"Do you have to wear that thing?" I finally asked him.

He acted like he didn't know what I was talking about.

"The T-shirt."

"It's a fuckin' T-shirt," he replied.

"You know what I mean. It's got Harvard on it in ten-foot letters."

"Afraid someone'll take your picture? Afraid Mommy's gonna see what you've come to?"

"It is the teensiest bit ostentatious," Louisa offered. "Perhaps even pretentious."

"It's not pretentious," Paul countered. "I went there."

I let it drop. I was too embarrassed to truly ask him not to wear it. I didn't want to admit how incredibly uncomfortable it made me. It marked us as outsiders. I don't know why, but those letters, H-A-R-V-A-R-D, declared our estrangement from everyone around us, these prototypical Americans with mall hair and cheap shoes. Paul seemed to revel in the distinction it gave him. Me... I didn't want them to know. My kind, we owned, we controlled, but we didn't let them know that. I was rich and that word unmasked me to the world, told them all the things about me that I'd leapt at this trip to erase—that I was wealthy and privileged and had done nothing to deserve any of it, that I slummed among the proles who shopped thrift stores from necessity, instead of irony, hoping their vaunted everyman inner light would burn away the artifice and release the kernel of the person I should have been.

It bothered me that Paul and Louisa treated this as an interlude, a temporary interruption in their lives-as-planned, whereas I wanted indelible transformation. Louisa bought items predicting their rarity back in the real world. And Paul saw little out here, little to learn. I envied them their relative comfort in their own skins and at the same time wanted to revile them for blindness and complacency, for not seeing the need to change everything. Condemning them would have been a comfort. It would have solidified my faith that my path was honest, my aim true. Unfortunately I couldn't, and I continued to regard their lack of desire for a revision of the world as a subtle rebuke of mine.

Campaign billboards and radio news jabbered on about the coming election and it seemed so apt—that the country I had chosen this particular moment to examine, to embrace, would obsess on renewal. "Let's Make America Great Again," the billboards blared with pictures of Reagan and Bush beaming down, simultaneously presuming historical greatness, its subsequent loss, and insisting that all it took was "Let's put on a show!" American gumption to bring it all back again. It just took will and a dream. That appealed to me. Not the politics, but the subtext.

I stopped the car at a big political rally in Arkansas. I saw a crowd of people and immediately knew what it was, but I wanted to see it up close. It was almost dusk and men were still making stump speeches. They must have been down to city councilmen by that time, but the crowd was healthy and red, white, and blue balloons, streamers, hats, and flags littered the ground below and the air above. The man on the "stump" shouted that it was time to take the country back, that the people in that crowd were the ones with the power to do it—people all over America just like them. He appealed to their belief in their own collective greatness. He appealed to their historically inviolate virtue. He marveled at their purity of heart. They, he said, were the soul of this City on the Hill. As he finished, the bad brass band blared while shouts and applause drowned them out. He left them rapt and screaming in a wash of rippling primary colors, certainty, and uprightness.

* * *

We did see some marvelous things. On a black night barely pierced by artificial headlights, smoke rose above the Arkansas hot springs. The earth itself smoldered. In the Smokey Mountains, I didn't hear a human sound. Not just an absence of voices, but nothing of, by, or for us. Leaves flashing autumn color floated to the rocky waters below. Trickling, chirping, rattling. A snake, a foraging squirrel, a beaver on the creek, that's all you heard—a creatures' world in which I was, again, an alien—again in a place that seemed familiar yet foreign and strange. What was and therefore should have seemed natural, like home, was instead a place I would never belong. Evolutionarily or personally, it was just too late for that.

We detoured through the strange landscape of southern Tennessee and northern Alabama. Here, it grew eerie. Paul had made fun of parts of Virginia and gaped at trailer parks called "Eden Estates," but this was an order of different magnitude. This was not the outskirts of the world I knew. This was another world altogether. I tried to separate my preconceptions from the reality I saw, but I don't know if that was possible. Wars mark places, and this one had been brutally scarred. I had visited battlegrounds in Europe and felt similar. Hell, you felt it in Paris—the remembrance of which rifle-wielding boots clattered against the cobblestones all those years ago. In Germany, it was omnipresent; I visited Buchenwald and the Wall. But there was acknowledgment there. It had been absorbed and it had been acceded to. Driving in my own country, though, it was different. There was no acknowledgment. Confederate flags waved on government buildings, front porches, and baseball caps. The ramifications of the fact that a war had been waged, fought, and lost here sat as oppressive as the clouded sky and the dank, humid air beneath it and as undigested as a swallowed stone. They sold postcards of confederate statues as if the renegades and losers deserved the paradise of marbleized eternity.

We took a detour to see the Cathedral Caverns. I'd seen pictures that amazed me and I wanted to be surrounded by them. I wanted to feel their grandeur all around me. If the world were ever to speak up and confess to the 'whys' and 'hows' of living in it, I figured these majestic eruptions of rock and void might be its voice. I tried to describe them to Paul and Louisa, but my words were insufficient to project what I'd seen in those photos; plus they weren't sharing my newfound 'nature boy' enthusiasm for the spiritually uplifting potential of flora, fauna, and natural wonders.

"Sounds like a bunch o' drippy rocks," Paul scoffed.

"It is," I confessed, "but they're huge and it had to take ages for the caverns to form and deform like that."

"Sounds neat," Louisa shrugged with a 'might as well see that as anything else' air.

Stopping outside a town near the attraction, we ducked into a store that looked like it majored in the tourist trade. We needed snacks and a bathroom. I noticed three men huddled at the corner of the counter listening to a radio. Their brows wrinkled in concentration and they leaned in close so that they didn't miss a word. I stopped to listen. There was a lot of inveighing against the evils of Godlessness embodied in welfare, feminists, and liberals along with paeans to an America once pure and blameless because it hewed to biblical basics and put its hand on its heart for the Pledge of Allegiance. The listening men occasionally glanced at one another and lifted their eyebrows or bobbed their heads in taciturn agreement. And then he said:

> *Our country aches, and every American who cares for her must, by now, feel her pain, for she lies in mortal peril. Do you hear those sounds? It's not progress; it is not freedom. It's neither of those things that real Americans hold so dear. No. It is our moral foundations creaking, for a rot eats away at them. Only you, Christian men and women, can stem it. Only you can save this great republic. The liberals will not help you. Hands over their ears, they will say they hear nothing of creaking foundations. They will say they smell no decay. Like pornographers and those who corrupt and prey on youth, they see no evil; and in their willful blindness, they spread it instead. Moral, Christian Americans must fight fiercely. This is a battle for America's soul, worthy of no lesser sacrifice than our bodies and our lives. This is our land, and we must save her from those who would tear her down, deny her glory and ours, and paint her small.*

A call to arms. A knowable divide between righteousness and corruption bound to absolute certainty regarding who funneled into which category, and I almost envied those men their ability to nod along and feature themselves among the former. I didn't listen anymore.

It was a strange, dark place we passed through en route to the Cathedral Caverns. They were quite beautiful, and maybe it was the radio preacher bleeding into it, but like the quiet in the Smokey Mountains, they awed, but this time to an unsettling degree, the forces and power they bespoke—the earth and its eons—so grand as to laugh and point mockingly at us mere men and our notions of order and right that puled from our crêpe papered rostrums and shop radios. I walked the railed passageway constructed to shield us from experiencing the true depths and dangers. Rock melted, stacked, stretched, and dripped in caverns enormous enough to house Titans—and as I looked at them, they sniggered. My insubstantiality had never seemed so palpable. This quest to end it never so important.

I sometimes think I willed it—the good and the bad—because I wanted something—something, anything momentous—so desperately. It's vainly satisfying to think I had the power to do that, that what happened was more than a chaotic series of random events. Even today, I long to think I drew it to me like a magnet. It would still be nice to think I mattered that much. I wanted to matter.

* * *

We left the angry, remorseless South for the relentless Midwest. When an endless strip of road numbs you with its sameness, there's nothing to do but stomp on the gas. We cut to Route 64 for a more northerly route through Oklahoma, but nothing changed. The flat, treeless, dun-colored world continued, purgatorily. We joked that the nothingness might never end. Could this be death? A quick check of the map promised more of the same whether we stuck with the panhandle or cut through northern Texas. So we risked a Midwest prison by doing 90—all day and all through the night.

It was my turn to drive. I had slept some during the day so I didn't think I was that tired, not until my head jerked up to see the center line smack beneath the car. After that, I concentrated on the radio to keep awake. Avoiding the preachers diverted me for a while. They were everywhere. I had seen TV parodies but only on this trip had I heard the real thing. They had amused until I'd seen the three men in Alabama nod to the litany of the damned with call to arms. They all went martial in the end, and most of the people on earth probably fell into one of their categories of the damned, so it came down to nihilism in the name of the Lord, again, as always, and that was too frightening traveling a strange, dark road at night; so I twirled on down the radio dial. Pop songs twittered on top 40 and the country stations twanged with affectations sufficient, in my green capsule shooting through the dark, to convince me that I, too, might be a cowboy.

As the sky lightened, I was beat. Louisa slept in the back in an elaborate nest she'd created from pillows we'd picked up along the way plus her haul of clothing and textile goods. She was practically cocooned. Paul had curled up in the front, his mouth slightly open and his head on a pillow smashed against the window.

We had a half a tank of gas, but I stopped anyway. Why this time? Why here? I had never stopped before we hit a quarter tank. Lots of good reasons, and yet none at all. I didn't want to drive anymore; I needed a break and didn't want to wake the others; I liked the look of the place. Whatever the reason, I stopped here, and it all began.

The place certainly caught the eye. The station loomed up in a pre-dawn haze like a giant insect. A fifties product, its bat-like wings stretched up into the mist, lined with yellow fluorescent light stretched out like veins. The recessed office sat in blue-gray darkness. I could barely see it. The moment I stopped, I leaned my head back against the seat and closed my eyes. I could have audibly sighed, it felt so good. After a moment, during which I fell asleep, a knock on the windshield startled me. My eyes jolted open to an attendant's maniacal grin sideways through the front windshield. Fumbling for the control, I hit the window switch. The long-faced, skinny attendant literally stuck his nose through the growing crack with the rest of his face following. I leaned backwards in alarm at the invasion of my space.

"What can I do for you, sir!" he practically shouted, expanding his crazed grin. Only this time, his eyes rolled this way and that as if in silent seizure. Alabama was nothing compared to this.

"Uh… fill it up, and, uh, could you check the oil and water, too?"

"Yes, sir!" he shouted, continuing to flick his eyes and then his head as if stricken with a tic.

He seemed reluctant to move from the window, but finally did. I leaned my head back again and heard the nozzle settle into position and the pump's meter clinking. A slap at the windshield opened my eyes to soapy water dripping from a filthy rag the attendant sloshed around. He still looked me right in the eye and he started muttering something

I couldn't hear. Again, he looked behind him, toward the office with increasing panic, and began to mutter a song.

"Desperado, why don't you come to your senses…"

Then he sang more audibly, but still tight lipped, as if practicing ventriloquism. He almost imperceptibly shook his head up and down at me, his trademark tic on fire. My eyes widened in wonderment. I was sure I witnessed full-fledged madness. Not daring to take my eyes off of him, I threw my hand out, smacking Paul.

"Is this guy weird or what?" I said.

"Ow." Paul moaned, shifted, and plopped his sleeping head on my lap.

I pushed him upright.

"Wha…?" He cast his half-masted eyes around and leaned toward my opened window.

"What's goin' on?"

"Your breath is foul," I informed him.

Like a diver, Paul hurled his body toward the back seat and rumbled through the wreckage.

The attendant insistently sang in his wooden whisper. *"Won't you let somebody love yooouuuu!"*

"What is his problem?" Paul asked, still on his knees in the front seat. He yanked on something in the back that seemed to yank back. He then sprawled backwards into the dashboard, his prize, a backpack, in hand.

"Ow!" Louisa cried, rising.

"You better let somebody love you, before it's too late…" the attendant positively hissed.

"Oh my God!" she cried, eying him. "Who is he? Where are we?" She whipped frantically around to stare through each window.

"We're at a gas station," I replied. "This guy's in another reality altogether."

"I can't get this door open."

I lifted my foot and gave Paul a healthy shove. The door opened and he spilled onto the ground.

"Thanks," he deadpanned. He stood up, brushed himself off, and headed toward where he assumed the bathrooms might be.

The attendant shut up. I saw the gun.

The attendant dropped the rag. His hands shot up in the air. The gunman leveled the metal somewhere between me and the attendant.

"How many people you got in there, huh?"

I didn't say anything. I didn't move. I considered putting my hands in the air, but I was too scared.

"Everybody out," he said.

As I swung my door open, taking pains to keep my hands visible, I dropped the attendant a seriously dirty look. Louisa climbed out the back.

"Idiot. Whatja think I was tryin' to tell you?" the attendant sneered at me, hands in the air.

"That you were an asshole with a lousy voice," I muttered back.

"Who you callin' an asshole, you little faggot!" He gave me a two-armed shove.

"Macho games," Louisa offered as I surprised myself and shoved back. "My fave."

"Knock it off!" the gunman screamed, waving the gun. "You're spillin' the gas over there."

Gas poured down the side of the car and snaked along the pavement. The attendant rushed to yank the nozzle from the tank. As he did, Paul walked out of the haze. The gunman's back to him, I wanted to warn him, but the gunman was looking right at me. I couldn't do anything.

"Uh, Ms. Merman," Paul snarked, "Could I get a key to the loo?"

The gunman backed up to include Paul in his range.

"Wow!" Paul exclaimed on seeing the gun, "I've never seen one that looked this real," and he rushed toward it.

"It IS real!" I choked out.

"What the fuck!" yelled the gunman. "Get outta here."

"It *is* real," I repeated.

"Geez. What's goin' on?" Paul asked.

"He's holdin' the place up is what's goin' on," the attendant answered.

"You got any rope?" the gunman asked.

"The trunk," Paul blurted.

"Jesus Christ!" Louisa spat.

Paul winced.

"You're dumber'n I am," the gunman chuckled. "Get it out and tie up this guy here." He waved the gun toward to the attendant.

Paul moved as slowly as possible to the trunk, and I moved as slowly as possible to pop it. As we all watched Paul stall and rummage, initial shock dissipated and I looked at the gunman instead of the gun.

He was young. He looked tired, so maybe on first, shocked blush he'd looked older, but I saw now that he was young. Sixteen young. He wore jeans that were too big and a red cotton zip-up jacket, somewhat faded, with a tan T-shirt underneath. His hair was really short, like a military buzz cut going to seed. It looked odd on someone so young. What had first appeared to be lines on his face were dirt. His face was dirty.

Paul pulled his head from the trunk and displayed the rope. He walked to the attendant, who reluctantly turned his back and put his arms behind him. Paul tied his hands and looked at the gunman, who flicked his gun toward the ground. Paul then bent down and tied the attendant's ankles together.

"Now… you start hoppin' down the road."

The attendant regarded him with open-mouthed outrage.

"Go on!" the gunman yelled.

The attendant took the first absurd hop. It was funny, but I didn't feel like laughing. He hopped again and soon bounced away into the mist as fast as his bound legs could carry him.

"Now, the rest of you get in the front seat," he ordered.

"I really gotta piss," Paul pleaded.

"Then piss."

Paul eyed the ground warily, and then shuffled to the side of a gas pump. We waited. In the surrounding silence it sounded like a waterfall. I slipped behind the wheel and Louisa sat beside me. As Paul zipped and arranged himself, the gunman impatiently waved his gun toward the car. Once we were in front, the gunman climbed in the back. Paul slammed the door, and in the rearview mirror, I saw the gunman slump with relief, as if he'd been holding his breath. He pulled cigarettes from his jacket pocket and lit one, inhaling deeply.

"Let's go," he said, as he threw the match out the window.

I started the car and pulled away. I continually stole glances in the rearview mirror. I could have sworn his lips moved as if he were talking to or arguing with himself. Anger welled up in me as I stared at him. That his hunk of metal gave him the right to tell me what to do pissed me off. Driving away, I started to seethe. Then a flash caught my eye. A yellow flash. I whipped around. Fire. All heads turned to see flames dance where the car had sat. We watched the flames engulf a gas pump.

I floored it. Necks whipped back as the car shot forward. The explosion punched like concurrent smacks to both ears. Projectiles soared through the air like fireworks. Octopus limbs made of flame shot from the black and orange fireball that displaced the gas station. We stared, amazed. Tires rattled on the shoulder of the road as I almost lost control.

"Oops," Paul whispered.

"Jesus. Wow," said the gunman.

It didn't register at the time—the magnitude of it. We were soon miles away. It happened 'back there.' I drove on as if I had witnessed a particularly colorful car wreck. The idea that we were being described to police or fireman didn't occur to me. Authorities never entered my mind. There were more pressing things at hand. My only concern was the gun pointed at me.

The gunman turned from the spectacle behind us as the fires shrank to nothing in the background. He sat facing forward in his seat, quiet for the longest, most unnerving time. I looked ahead at the road, too scared to glimpse left or right, dreading.

"Where you folks headed?" he asked in a dissonantly innocent tone.

I didn't know if I should lie, so I went vague. "West," I replied.

He shot another glance out the rear windshield. Speaking into the glass, he said, "You mind if I come along?"

Simultaneously, Louisa, Paul and I eyed one another, confounded.

"Sure."

"Nope."

"Not at all."

"Fine."

"Your call."

"Love the company," Paul had to add.

General dismay all around. In the rearview mirror, he seemed to take our assent to heart. He looked satisfied and shook his head up and down as if pleased with the turn of events.

"Where were you headed?" I asked.

"Where you all from?" he asked as if he hadn't heard me.

"Back east." Again, I kept it vague. I don't know why. I just thought I should.

"Yeah. That's where. Someplace like that," he said as if I'd stumbled on the answer he'd been seeking. "Someplace big."

"Big's not all it's cracked up to be," I added, trying to sound humble, and, I must admit, defending my 'truth in mid-Americana' dreamings, already under assault from Paul, Louisa, and mounting experience.

"Better'n here," he replied. "Gotta be. Ain't nothin' out here." He looked angry. "Just a bunch o' assholes think they know somethin'… Don't know shit. They all talk about how it used to be an' what they used to do and how they use to live and cuss out folks on TV 'cause it ain't that way no more… can't make a livin' anymore… blah blah blah. I don't give a shit how it used to be or what people thought it was gonna be… I just know there ain't nothin' left, and it ain't my fault."

I shrugged for lack of anything to say. "Hard times," popped out, which I regretted immediately.

"I hate it here."

I didn't ask why.

"My name's Jesse," he said, anger still in his voice.

He leaned forward and reached out his hand to shake. Stupefaction does not describe it. I was unnerved, disarmed, insulted, intrigued… but I shoved a hand awkwardly upward like a school kid and allowed him to rattle it around. When finished, he pushed his hand at Louisa, who, mouth agape, followed suit. On his turn, Paul practically tore his hand away the moment skin met skin.

The gunman… no. That sounds wrong now. He wasn't anymore. He was not a man. Gunboy? Boy with gun? Armed teen? At that point,

I didn't know what he was. More to the point, I didn't know how much of a danger to regard him.

"What you all goin' west for?" he asked.

"Same as you," I replied. "Get away." Perhaps his opening up and the handshake softened me, but I added, "You know… shake things up a bit."

"Yeah," he grinned broadly. "Shake things up."

I don't know why that amused him. "California's as far as you can go, right?" he asked.

Paul leaned forward to present me with his 'what the fuck' expression.

"Yeah," I answered, ignoring Paul. "Pretty much. Without a boat."

"Sounds like a good place, then."

We drove in silence. Of course, I had never faced a gun before. The reactions came in waves. At first, I was scared, then pissed. Seeing it pointing at me, I tasted my own powerlessness. If I could have willed the hand holding that gun to die slowly and painfully, I would have. I never forgot the gun, but my anger had abated. He was more of a person now and less an appendage of the gun. He sat in the back of my car looking nervously, restlessly out the windows, desperate to be elsewhere. I didn't know if he wanted release from a place or from himself, but either way, it gripped me. I couldn't fail to see that he hurt, and that his quest might abstrusely mirror mine.

I wanted to know more: where did he come from, what was he running from, who did he want to be? But with a boy sitting alone in a voluminous back seat, gun cradled in his lap, there were no words. Everything that came to mind suggested pain, which I did not want to trigger in anyone so young and armed.

Again we drove in silence. I watched the dashboard clock slip forward. Outside, the haze lifted as the sun slowly climbed its way up on the world.

"Let me see the map," I said.

Paul reached into the glove compartment.

"Whoa," Jesse grunted, straightening and lifting his gun.

"I just want to see the map," I soothed. "Shortest way to get there." He looked at my eyes in the mirror. Satisfied, he relaxed.

Not wanting to spook our guest, Paul handed Louisa the map so slowly and with such care it might have been a grenade. She opened it and located our position on the Oklahoma panhandle. This endlessly flat land with a straight black and yellow line running through it had always given me the creeps. I could see why he wanted out. I chose north. I sped through the vast nothing, fleeing a landscape shrieking of purposelessness, mocking with its majestic desolation. There was a boy with a gun in my car—scared, and the scared are dangerous; he did not need to be mocked.

I tried to ignore the perpetual frantic hand dances in Paul's and Louisa's laps. I don't think they understood the half of what they were trying to signal each other. Louisa repeatedly cast me heavy glances, as if awaiting her overdue rescue. These, too, I ignored. There was nothing to say. There was nothing I could do. I drove.

After three hours of quiet, my stomach finally spoke. "I need to eat," I declared as confidently as I could. In the mirror, Jesse didn't immediately respond. After a while, though, he nodded his head. I checked what would have been a loud exhalation, realizing I'd been holding my breath since breaching the silence.

The first restaurant I saw after pulling off the highway didn't have a drive-through window. That meant we had to eat inside. Could have been good; could have been bad. In public, perhaps we could turn him in; sitting in a 'normal' setting might humanize us to him, or him to us; it might let us talk to him and find out what he was about. But then again, being in public might spook him. Someone might see the gun and react, setting him off. Yes, he was armed, but I feared his fear more than anything else. It was just a sense I got.

I didn't know the right thing to do. I proceeded anyway. Ignoring a decidedly elevated heartbeat drumming on my temples, I parked in front of the restaurant awaiting the worst, taking it second by second. *Okay,* I told myself after each action, *no reaction yet. Nothing yet.* Turn the wheel. *Nothing yet.* Hit the brake. *Nothing yet.* Turn off the ignition. *Nothing yet.* Open the door. *Nothing yet.*

Standing outside the car, he seemed understandably nervous at the public place and the people, but not explosive. I relaxed. I decided we'd live long enough to eat something.

Entering the restaurant, I wondered if he—this *gun-teen*—was what awaited me. I had taken this trip to say, "I'm here. Have at me. Show me what you got." I had arrogantly thought the world had plans for me; it just needed to know that I was willing. Could this disheveled kid with his hunched shoulders and resentful eyes have been the Fates' answer to my childish dare? He had dropped squarely in my path, like a piano falling on the sidewalk. At that huge a circumstance, you look for a reason. I examined him more closely now. Perhaps he was the embodiment of a need or a want that I didn't even know I had. Perhaps he was me—without the grooming and pretensions (if such a thing could have possibly existed).

Jittery, Jesse stopped outside the restaurant door. He looked through the glass. The place was half-full. Not enough bodies to trigger anxiety, I thought, but enough to blend into.

I did not see the little girl staring out the window.

"Looks okay," I said.

I pulled the door open and let the others through. Jesse entered last, hands jammed in his red windbreaker pockets, the right of which, I knew, held the gun. He leaned his back against the door to let me pass in front of him.

I approached Louisa as the uniformed waitress pulled four menus from her podium and motioned us toward a booth against the front window. "Okay?" I silently asked Jesse. He nodded imperceptibly. I gestured Louisa to sit.

She and Paul took one side of the booth. Jesse sat beside me on the other. Our eyes darted randomly to avoid one another's. I snapped my menu open. As if permission had been conferred, Louisa and Paul opened theirs, thankful for something to do. Jesse, too, raised his.

After a moment, he ran his finger horizontally along the plastic menu. His lips moved slightly. I wondered how well he could read. I was tempted to offer help, but I didn't dare; I didn't want to embarrass him.

"I always get pancakes when I go to a place like this," I said. Paul and Louisa squinted at the lie, but I thought a kid might consider them a treat. After perusing the menu a few moments longer, Jesse shook his head in assent.

"Yeah."

I folded my menu and laid it down. Jesse watched me and did the same.

"You all ready?" the waitress asked as she passed. We ordered. Jesse went last, and when the waitress looked at him, he didn't say anything. He looked at us, at her, as if we all sat accusing him instead of waiting for his order.

"He'll have pancakes," I said. The waitress looked at Jesse for assent, but he didn't look back. I shook my head in emphasis as I handed back the menus and she went on her way.

Waiting for the food was the worst. Louisa removed her jacket, then Paul followed, revealing his Harvard T-shirt. I closed my eyes in irritated disbelief and glared daggers at him. That's the way to keep low-key: prance around Cribdeath, Utah blaring a Harvard sign.

"What is that?" Jesse immediately asked about the huge letters and logo covering Paul's chest.

"It's a school," I answered.

"You all go there?"

"Yeah. Went."

"Why'd you stop?"

"Graduated."

"Where is it?"

"It's in Massachusetts," I said. "Outside Boston."

"I heard of it, I think. It's special, right?"

"A special needs school," Louisa muttered, stuffing a smile.

"It's well-known," I replied.

"I didn't graduate."

"You must be too young," I said.

"How old are you?" he asked.

"Twenty-one."

"You're in high school and twenty-one?" He screwed up his face in disbelief.

"No," I smiled. "College. We graduated from college."

"Oh. Mine was high school. I left. They said it wasn't gonna do me no good anyway. I thought they'd try to make me stay, but they didn't."

"Didn't your parents try to make you?"

"A lot of it didn't make sense to me," he continued, ignoring the question, and with increasing passion. "Half the times, I'd hear the words, but it was like they were never there. Know what I mean? Like there'd be one thing and that was okay. But then there'd be another, and they'd say that it was like the first thing or more of it and put 'em together; but I didn't get it. They acted like it was my fault. Like I didn't want to or didn't try. I did, though. It wasn't my fault."

Paul's and Louisa's eyes analyzed the tabletop Formica. I felt the first stirring of pity. He stared at us—from one to the other—terrified and expectant, as if this was his test for us, and for him.

"Lots of folks have that happen," I shrugged, trying to sound nonchalant. "Some don't process information like other people. It doesn't mean they aren't smart or can't learn. They just need to do it a different way."

I could tell he wasn't sure if this was what he wanted. He wasn't sure if we had passed the test. But I saw relief on his face, suggesting it would do. He smiled at me and tried to share it with Paul and Louisa. Both were stagily preoccupied with pouring coffee from the carafes on the table.

"I used to get a lotta ribbin' about it," he added.

The waitress arrived and distributed plates from her tray. As she disappeared, she tossed back a perfunctory, "You all enjoy your meal."

Jesse poured quantities of syrup on his pancakes and clutched his fork in a fist. He lowered his mouth to the food as opposed to raising the food to his mouth.

"I need to go to the bathroom," Louisa said as she shooed Paul out of the booth.

"Uh-uh." Jesse's head shot up as his fork clanged to his plate. His eyes darted back and forth as if snatching the lay of the land before staring back down at the table. I felt the gun press against my inner thigh. I violently shook my head at Louisa. "Sit!" I told her. The gun trembled against me.

"It's okay," she stammered. "I just need…"

"Not here," Jesse muttered to his plate, swallowing.

"Okay," she said, almost lifting her hands in the air before she thought better of it.

"You can go on the road," Jesse told her, trying to appease.

"I didn't mean anything," she said, lifting her fork to poke at her omelette.

The pressure on my leg receded. Again, we ate in silence, but Jesse, head half-buried in his plate, nonetheless kept raising his eyes and openly studying us.

"You all must be good friends," he said.

"Yeah," I nodded. "We've known each other a long time."

"Guess I never knowed nobody long enough."

At that, he concentrated on his food until the waitress arrived with the check.

"You all enjoy your meal?" she asked as she scribbled without setting eyes on any of us.

"Fine," I replied.

She slapped the bill down.

"Not now!" we heard from the adjacent booth. A little head suddenly floated above the back of the booth behind Paul and Louisa. The girl, who looked about eight or nine, held a book in her hand as if she'd just been reading. She canvassed each of us—and each plate and, seemingly, each utensil—with thoroughness and bald inquiry, as if we were the first people and food she'd ever seen. She smiled at Jesse and he smiled back—a big, blatant smile displaying lots of syrup-smeared teeth. He looked like one child grinning at another. Even with the grin, his dirty face was neither appealing nor unappealing. I realized what had seemed odd about it: it did not bespeak malice, intelligence, big-heartedness, dullness, or kindness. It did not elicit sympathy or ill will or any other identifiable response. It was empty, as if nothing had yet been imprinted on it. I thought back on my own face five years ago and thought that there must have been something essential there, a whisper of who I was or might become. I saw nothing essential in Jesse's, and it unnerved me. One second, he smiled and was a child. The next, he pointed a gun with a man's conviction. I couldn't find a thread from one to the other.

The girl kneeling on the adjacent bench was all wishful curiosity. Even her smile probed, as if cataloguing our reactions to it.

Paul and Louisa craned their necks to see the floating head behind them.

"Hello there," Louisa chirped.

The girl didn't respond. She took the opportunity to study Paul's and Louisa's newly visible faces.

"What's your name?" Louisa continued.

A woman's voice snapped, "Cindy, turn around and sit down. Stop bothering those people." The girl's body jerked before she disappeared; a rough hand had grabbed her. "Look at you," the woman carped. "Go on and wash up."

I saw her gnomish figure scuttle from the booth clutching her little book and head toward the bathrooms. She looked back at us as she did.

And then a man's voice came from Cindy's booth, angry enough to negate his attempts at a whisper: *"Just don't talk about it in front of her."*

"Why not? She's coming with me." The woman didn't even try to keep it down; she was pissed and didn't care if the whole world heard.

I did not see Louisa sneak a pen from her purse or Paul purloin a paper napkin. Beneath the table, as I listened, Louisa scribbled a note.

"What for? So you can dump her in that damned school and forget about her?"

"I wouldn't have to 'dump her in that school' if you had some spine!"

"You gonna ruin her to punish me?"

"Show me a better way."

I didn't want to hear any more. "Let's go."

"I'll take care of it," Louisa announced, grabbing the bill. That should have raised alarms, but the fight in the next booth still singed my ears. I thought about unwantedness; about loneliness. The two seemed particularly present right then.

Louisa lagged behind as she pulled bills from her purse. Jesse stopped to wait.

"I need some change," Louisa called.

Paul dashed to the table, pulling coins from his pocket. Together, they left the bill, the money, and, unbeknownst to me, a note. Only later did I learn of it. It read: *Help. We're hostages. Call police.*

No one knew what happened to that note. Louisa asked. She asked the cops. She even called the restaurant. No one had seen it. I imagine the waitress clearing up, grabbing her money and calculating the tip we'd left, mechanically sucking up all the breakfast debris, of which a scribbled-up napkin that might have saved a life was just another speck.

* * *

Jesse opened the passenger door. He should not have been able to; I hadn't yet put the key in my lock. "These doors aren't working," I said. "Jesse. Can you close the door?" After he did so, I locked the doors again. Again, he opened his. "Used car," I shrugged.

We resumed our positions—me in the driver's seat, Paul on the passenger side, and Louisa in the middle. Again, Jesse took the back. The time in the restaurant had only inflamed my curiosity. I peered at the back seat through the rearview mirror as much as I looked at the road.

"What about your folks, Jesse? Won't they be looking for you?"

He barely shrugged, gazing at the nothing out the window.

"They must miss you. Must wonder where you are."

No response. I didn't try again. We drove. At least the relentlessly featureless landscape transformed itself the farther west we got. It stopped screaming stasis and started doing what I so cravenly wanted—it started murmuring promises. Slight undulations lifted the road, and little dots of green littered the land alongside. Then came a national park with bona fide hills and valleys, sprouting evergreens, offering the opportunity to imagine wonders just over this rise, or the next. The Long March through the flat, dank Valley of Dread came to an end. This was the Yellow Brick Road. You knew it led somewhere, and it let you dream that somewhere to be wonderful. Spirits lifted. I felt it. Paul and Louisa, fear aside, smiled through the windows at the world despite themselves. Paul rolled down his window to smell the air. No one objected. Jesse roamed the back seat like a squirrel trying to take it all in.

After another look at the map, I took a chance. I cut north and found a road nestled between plateaus, as if cupped in gods' hands. As we turned onto 163, huge formations loomed, sentry-like, welcoming or warning, I couldn't tell. Colors I never dreamt occurred in nature flashed in the sunlight, no longer dirt brown or mere green grass, but elaborately painted earth. And then a long, straight stretch of road with giant headstones in the distance. Again, it looked like Titans had died here and marked their time and place with flamboyantly mountainous stone caps, towering over eternity and guaranteeing that we'd never forget. It was just as forbidding as the barren landscapes we had traveled. Those vast chasms of featureless space had screamed relentless futility, as if designed by gods disgusted with their subjects and determined to display it with a landscape both mirroring and mocking their empty vanity. This place also screamed our insignificance, but without malice. There was no bitterness in this new landscape. It did not suggest its own disillusionment with us. Savagely disgruntled gods didn't leave it behind. The gods of this land did not hold us in contempt. They may well have taken pity on us. I could look on it without disgrace, and therefore in honest wonder.

"I have to go to the bathroom."

I was sure I had heard it. Paul and Louisa looked as confused as I was. In the rearview mirror, I saw Jesse look down, then shriek as his feet flew up on the seat as if he'd seen a snake.

"I have to go to the bathroom," the small voice insisted.

And then, in the mirror, the head emerged. I hit the brake so hard I practically ate the windshield. The car fishtailed as it careened to the shoulder. I flung my door open and leapt out. Everyone else tumbled after. We stared at the car as if expecting it to talk. Instead, the little girl emerged, immediately recognizable from the restaurant.

"I have to go to the bathroom," she repeated pleadingly. I stood disbelieving. I could not move. Nobody did. Finally, Louisa defied the enormous gravity of yet more shock. She leaned into the car and snagged a box of tissues, grabbed the girl by the hand and marched with her into the distance.

The rest of us stood like mannequins. Paul was the first to reanimate.

"Oh, SHIT!" he screamed. "I don't *believe* this." He started pacing, his hands to his head. "What are we gonna do? Oh, shit!"

I shrugged and shook my head in unnecessary and unproductive gestures of incredulity.

"She's kinda cute," Jesse said.

"Jesus Christ! That doesn't mean we get to keep her, now, does it?" Paul spat. "We gotta take her back."

Jesse backed up and placed his hand in his jacket pocket. I gestured for Paul to settle down.

"Paul," I said. He wasn't listening. He kept pacing and stuttering "Oh, shit!" as if finally permitted to vent all of his fear and frustration. "Paul!" I shouted. He looked at me, and I nodded toward Jesse with his hands in his red jacket pockets, one clearly bulkier than the other. Paul got the point. "It's a couple of hundred miles," I said.

Jesse shook his head from side to side. "They mus' be lookin' for me," he said. "I can't go back."

"That's not our fault," Paul snapped.

Jesse looked hurt, and then angry.

"Be quiet, Paul."

"Why? So we can all pretend we're buds?"

"Paul..."

"You defending him now?"

"Shut up, Paul. Just shut the fuck up." I couldn't believe him. I tried to burn some sense into him with my eyes, to melt whatever made him think antagonism was helpful here.

"We still goin' to California, right?" Jesse asked, ingenuous.

Paul stared at me, daring me, but I had no choice.

"Yeah. Yeah," I assured. "We're just gonna stay around here for the night."

At that, Jesse looked relieved. He relaxed the hand in the jacket pocket.

Louisa and the little girl returned. Louisa paused at the tension. "Everything okay?" she asked.

"Yep," I chirped.

"Okay. This is Cindy. These guys are Lennie and Paul."

"Hello," Cindy said.

"And this is Jesse," I added, much to Paul's disgust.

"Hello," the girl repeated, as Jesse gave a little wave.

"And why is Cindy with us?" Paul asked.

"She saw us arrive at the restaurant," Louisa said. "Right?" Cindy nodded. "Picked us out the moment we pulled up. Aren't we lucky?"

"Where the hell was she?" I asked, as if the girl wasn't there.

"She buried herself under all the crap in the back."

I shelved all of my questions. Everything buzzed and jangled. There was too much going on and I didn't have time to assess it, much less plan a way out of it. We needed to talk. We needed Jesse settled. We had to get the girl home.

"There was a sign for a state park back a few miles." I just started talking and hoping for the best, as if words alone would save us. "We can set up and stay around the park for the night, right?" Noting the worry on Jesse's face, I added, "We'll find an out-of-the-way place. No people around. It'll be safe."

No one objected.

"You can ride in the back with me," Jesse said to Cindy with a playmate's brightness, his hand still on the gun in his pocket.

She clamored into the back. As she did, Jesse transformed again. Just for a moment, he looked at us, and in his eyes—momentarily a man's eyes—I could have sworn he was warning. Then he climbed in behind her.

Paul gritted his teeth and slammed his heavy door with everything he had as a final act of rebellion. We drove about 50 miles back the way we came. By this time, we'd grown used to uncomfortable silences. No one felt compelled to start a conversation. I never even considered the radio. Occasionally, someone would open a window or close one, increasing or diminishing the ambient noise, but silence became an escort. Three friends, two strangers, and silence, boxed and sealed, desperate to be apart, on a journey that needed to end but just plain refused.

I swept past the trailer park signs and even risked the transmission by driving off-road, but I found a nook protected by mounds on three sides. No one would see us there.

I stopped the car.

"I'm not gonna let you take me back." Cindy sat upright in the back seat, her high-pitched voice belying her grave countenance. Paul, Louisa, and I didn't even glance at one another on this one. We were beyond expressions of shock.

"Let's set up," I said, as I swung my door open and stepped into the desert.

* * *

"You ever been campin'?" Jesse asked Cindy, as they toted blankets, coolers, and sleeping bags from the car to the camping spot.

"Uh-uh," she replied.

"Me neither."

"Kinda fun, ain't it?"

Jesse took a moment, as if deciding. "Yeah," he answered.

Watching them, Louisa and I walked down to the car. "What are we gonna do?" she asked.

"Find a way to take her back."

"What do we do about him?"

I shook my head. "I don't know. Neither of 'em seem too keen on home. Sometimes he seems harmless."

"He held up a gas station. Kidnapped us at gunpoint."

"You know what I mean."

"No. I don't."

"Like he wouldn't hurt anybody. Like he doesn't mean to hurt us. Just sort of… messed up."

"So we do what? He's messed up, so we take him to California?"

"No."

"What, then?"

I attempted an impish smile.

"You're loving this, aren't you?" she accused, her face alight with realization. "It's pushing all your Cinemascope buttons. 'Bigger Than Life!' 'On the Lam!' 'Starring Lennie Ashland!' I can see the marquee now."

"I'm not the one making a big deal out of this," I insisted defensively. I almost walked away.

"It is a big deal," she said, as she grabbed my arm. "It's a *big deal*."

She had me cold, but part of me couldn't admit it. Romance was for sophomore girls. It was for the irrational, not the cultivated. It may have also been human, but that was no comfort. Shitting was human, but no one did it in public. I had an image of myself that I needed others to mirror back to me: strong, supremely rational, and above… yes, above the merely human. In my young mind, it was the only way to ennoble my little shred of a life, cursed as I was with needing it to be so much more.

Louisa looked behind her and there stood Cindy.

"If you're talking about taking me back, you can forget it. I can run away from you just as fast as I did back there."

Louisa and I exchanged exhausted airs.

"Where you headed?" Cindy asked.

"California," I acquiesced.

"They got palm trees there, don't they?"

"Yep."

"And an ocean."

"Uh-huh."

"I'm coming with you."

Louisa broke this time. She laughed despite herself, almost trembling with fury and the absurdity of it all. She grabbed Cindy and swung her in a wide arc. The girl trilled with glee as she grabbed Louisa's hand and dragged her to the campsite.

I have to admit I watched it all like play and with an inappropriate sense of familial pride at these disparate strains blending and bonding under my baton. Jesse approached Paul, who was fighting unnecessarily with a sleeping bag zipper.

"You need some help?" Jesse asked in a blatant attempt at fence mending. Paul intensified his struggle. He ignored Jesse, who slouched away with the look of deep injury that only a teenager could carry. He shook it off, though, when Cindy and Louisa pranced by.

"Hey, I'm comin' with you," the little girl shouted at him.

"Awright, kid!" he cried, running toward her. "You and me in California." He, too, picked her up and swung her around, to her delight. "When we see the ocean, I'll race you to it."

"I'll beat ya," she boasted.

"Oh yeah?"

"Yeah!"

Some of them were happy. Two for the first time in a while. On the grand desert floor, they frolicked like cats. They were content, and they looked to me like they belonged. This unearthly place accepted us. He had a gun and she had run away from God knows what and would have to go back to it, but the past vanished, and I felt some peace. The seemingly omniscient world that had vise-gripped me all of my life disappeared, along with its violent intrusions and unforgiving expectations, the ones that scattered my family, that crushed my father. The worlds we'd fled couldn't hurt us here. I felt like this lavish place protected us beneath its wing.

I was congratulating myself when Paul stormed toward me. "What the hell are you doin', telling her she's coming with us?"

"I didn't tell her," I chuckled, trying to make light of it. "She told us."

"It's just gonna make it that much harder to take her back," he railed.

"Who says we're taking her back?" I replied with sufficient jocularity to mask my growing anger.

"Oh. I see. You decide this all by yourself?"

"Come on, Paul. Lighten up."

"Lighten up? Are you crazy? This is kidnapping!"

"I'll take care of it."

"You forget your little friend has a gun."

"He's not going to hurt anybody."

"Oh, now he reads minds."

"Why are you being such an ass?"

"This is my life you're fucking with!"

I turned away from him, but he grabbed me and wheeled me around.

"What are you playing at?'

"It's no game," I hissed. I shook free and walked away. He followed, yelling. Everyone stopped to listen.

"You got some retard with a gun, add a little girl, a couple o' schmucks you drag along for the ride, the cops prob'ly after us…?"

"Nobody paid you to come along."

"Bullshit. Who waved the money around and said he'd take care of everything?"

"You didn't say no."

"No one's said no to you in your life."

"That's not my fault."

"You are scary! You don't give a shit about *anyone*, do you? As long as you get to play, what, outlaw? Savior?"

"YOU HAVE NO IDEA WHAT I WANT!" I screamed.

"TELL ME."

"You wanted this just as much as I did. Sentenced to that fucking black cart."

"It's called living. It's called *working*."

"It's called *waiting*. It's called *dying*."

"I'm not your Dad, Lennie. I got plenty o' time."

Jesse approached. "Hey," he said softy, but got no further.

"You SHUT UP," Paul pointed and hollered at him before he turned back on me.

"Why'd you bring us along, huh, me and her, an audience?" He pointed at Louisa.

"I got everything ready up there," Jesse interjected.

Paul shoved him. "Shut up. You don't get to talk."

I moved on Paul.

"This just fun and games to you?" He shoved Jesse again. "You like this? This fun?"

Looking more scared than anything else, Jesse put his hand in his pocket.

"Fun and games?" Paul shouted again.

I wheeled on Paul and shoved him against the car, my elbow on his neck. "Life and death," I hissed in his ear.

It felt as if everyone had heard and took one step back, aghast. We froze.

"Whose?" Paul finally whispered.

With that single word, I saw and heard myself. I backed off. Paul rubbed his neck in astonishment—probably at both of us—awaiting a response to a question, the source of which I couldn't fathom. I did not know why I had said it—"life and death." It had spewed from someplace I didn't control. The idea that I enjoyed the threat and danger, it astonished me, and I rejected it. I was trembling.

As Paul walked into the distance, I shook my head to clear it. I had invited nothing, I assured myself. I had prolonged nothing. I had simply reacted to circumstance. I said it again and again.

"Where's he going?" asked Louisa.

"Don't know."

"He comin' back?" Cindy queried, sidling up to Louisa.

"Don't know."

Louisa put her hand on my arm. "What did you say to him?"

I wanted to tell her, to confess what I'd said, but I couldn't. "C'mon," I said. "Let's go eat."

"Can I use his sleeping bag?" Cindy shouted with delight at the very idea.

"No!" Louisa snapped.

Calm returned. Me, Louisa, Jesse, and Cindy sat around a fire and ate beans from a can and roasted hot dogs on the fire. I saw flashes of the familial peace at which I'd marveled a little while ago, but it was tainted now. Watching them smiling and talking, laughing in front of me, I only saw doleful endings. My exchange with Paul, my outburst of... what... truth? Bluster? It put the lie to my daydreams. True to form, never a break from Paul, but this time, I didn't like it so much. It took real work to nurture the familial glow I thought I'd glimpsed here. Work I had not done. Fate seemed to be seriously dicking with me to manufacture this semblance of peace out of grotesquely mismatched pieces and tease me with what I hadn't the depth to mold. I acted in a satire of my longings; I was damned to acknowledge it.

When the food had been eaten, and Cindy sat braiding Louisa's hair, Jesse sat down beside me.

"My bein' around got him pretty mad, huh?"

"Yeah."

"I didn't do nothin' to him."

"I know," I reassured. "He just doesn't like… surprises."

"Good luck with that. I thought he was gonna come after me for a minute."

"You've got the gun, remember?"

"Yeah, but I ain't got no bullets for it."

At first he might have said, 'I am particularly fond of pears.' It took a moment to register.

"You're shitting me."

He turned that blank young face toward me. "Uh-uh," he shrugged, guilelessly.

I waited, staring at him, but he didn't say anything more.

"What?" I asked, incredulous.

He looked back, quizzically, as if I were slow. As I continued staring open-mouthed, he pulled the gun from his pocket. He offered it in the palm of his hand. "I took it from my Ma and I don't know where she keeps 'em."

I picked it up. I had never held one before. It was short with a round barrel. I fiddled with it, trying to get it open. Jesse helped, and when the barrel fell, the six round cylinders were empty. Dumbfounded, I handed the gun back to him.

I sunk my head in both hands and squeezed as hard as I could. It felt good. I dragged my fingers down my face as if trying to yank it off. I think I blubbered through clamped teeth and loose lips. I patted Jesse on the shoulder as I rose and walked toward the car. I don't know what I wanted there. Just to be alone, I think. I should have laughed, but I didn't. I sat on the passenger side and closed the door, sealing myself in. Leaning my head back, I shut my eyes. I sat there for some time.

It was almost dark by the time I opened my eyes. There hadn't been any sleeping, nor thinking to speak of. Instead, exhaustion seeped out of me, like a long sigh, and relief slipped in. Lifting my hand, I noticed the lingering tremor. Obviously, I had not confessed what this day had done to me.

Louisa approached as I stepped from the car. "The gun wasn't loaded," I spilled.

"Jesus Christ!"

She leaned forward, her hands on her knees. She puffed out a stunted laugh.

"Hey, Louisa," Cindy cried. "Come and read to us."

"Fuck," she said, ignoring the girl. "Why...?"

I didn't even let her finish. "I don't know. I guess he wanted money. He'd already brandished the gun at the station and just kept it up with us to get away."

"Well," she sighed. "That's over. At least the worst part of it. Now we just have to worry about her." She nodded toward Cindy.

"Tomorrow," I said.

"Come oonnnn!" Cindy wailed.

We headed back to the campsite.

"You scared the shit outta me with that empty gun," Louisa chastised Jesse as she settled on the ground.

"I'm sorry. I didn't know you folks would be cool. I didn't have money and I had to get away from there..."

She cut him off. "Yeah, yeah. Whatever."

Cindy ignored the book in her lap and stared instead at a small figurine she held—a delicately carved horse, impressive in detail, of finely grained wood.

"What's that?" Louisa asked.

"My dad gave it to me." Cindy stood and turned away as if to shield the figure from our eyes.

"You miss him?" Louisa asked.

Cindy shrugged.

"What about your mom?"

She suddenly wheeled toward us. "I know all about California," she exclaimed.

Louisa went with it. "Good. Then you can tell me. I don't know anything."

"They make movies there," Cindy said, stroking her figurine and pacing, one foot before the other as if walking a crack in the pavement. "They have earthquakes and the sun shines all the time."

Louisa picked up a flashlight and followed her. I sat down next to Jesse. I wanted to know everything. My curiosity raged, since I no longer feared a bullet. But he had something else on his mind.

"You ever get scared sometimes?" he asked.

It was an odd question. "Of what?" I asked.

"Sometimes I get scared," he replied. "I don't know why. Gets hard to breathe."

"Something must scare you," I said.

He screwed up his face. "Things. Regular things. School. People…" He clearly couldn't explain and stopped trying. "My Ma says I'm jus' crazy."

"You're not crazy." As soon as I said it I realized it was an assurance I couldn't honestly make. "Why'd you leave, Jesse?"

He picked up a rock and dug at the dirt, legs tucked up against him and his arms wrapped around. "Nothin' there. Nobody."

"You mentioned your mother."

He looked up at Louisa and Cindy. "She your girl?" he asked.

"Uh-uh," I replied.

"Why not? She's pretty. And real nice."

"She is. She's very pretty. And nice. We're very different." I looked at him, wondering if I should let the question about his mother go. He clearly didn't want to answer it. "What about you?" I asked. "You got a girl?"

"Nah," he smiled, resigned. "Girls never like me."

"What about your mother, Jesse?" I made myself ask again. The question was a formality, like 'how do you do?' I didn't want to know that badly. I felt I knew who he was, as if I didn't need the details. Perhaps I feared they'd squash some of the notions I had about him, create a flesh and blood reality out of my thin projection. But I knew I ought to ask, so I did. It was the responsible thing to do.

The question hung there. I let the silence sing for a while. He grew increasingly uncomfortable. I did nothing to change that.

"It's better if I ain't there," he said.

"Better for you?"

He stared at the dirt his finger picked at and shrugged.

"Wasn't much rain this year. Everyone was talkin' about that. She said it every day… 'No rain again…' like she was a farmer or somethin', but she jus' works in an office. When she went on like that means her church talked about it."

"Did you go with her… to church?"

He shook his head. "I did a few years ago, when she started, but I stopped. She says that's when I started goin' bad. You go?"

I shook my head.

"Don't you believe in God?" he asked.

"I doubt it," I replied, too clever by half.

"Ain't you scared o' goin' to hell?"

My first impulse was a smart-ass 'been there,' but I hadn't—far from it—and didn't have the right to joke about it. "Don't believe in that, either," I substituted, and as I did, felt a little smaller for my serial disbeliefs.

"She does," he continued. "She said she did wrong havin' me like she did. She said she had to make up for it and I did, too. She said we had to be really good."

"What do you mean 'how she had you'?"

"She didn't have a husband." He paused. "I'm supposed to say he's dead. That's what she told me to say and I always did, too. After a while, I had a whole story about him." He smiled. "He died savin' us, from a car crash. He pulled us out of a fire an' saved us." The smile slipped away. "That was good, huh, him doin' that? A good story."

I nodded. "Do you know your real father?"

"I asked her about him. She never told me. At first she said he was dead and that was it. Then when she got into the church she told me about her sinnin'. Said it was all right though 'cause God was the only father I needed and I had to please him or he'd turn his back on me and on her, that I had her fate in my hands so I had to please my one true father. But I knew I couldn't please him."

"Why?" I asked him.

Another patented shrug. Then he said it with a knowledge of hopelessness far beyond his years.

"How?"

His whole being bespoke the impossibility. How do you please God? If you couldn't please a parent or a teacher or even another kid in school, how the hell could you please an all-seeing, persnickety God? It would be useless to even try. It would be just a quantum magnification of already numerous and well-recorded failures.

"She almost married a guy a couple years ago," Jesse volunteered. "He was around a while. Longer'n any o' the others. She told me he was gonna be my father. He seemed okay, but he left. She cried a lot when he did. Then she got mad."

"You get mad when someone walks out on you," I told him.

"It was me. She wasn't mad at him. She was mad at me."

Again, I remained silent, thinking he'd say more. But he volunteered nothing. "How'd you make her mad?" I asked.

Again nothing. "What, Jesse?"

"Just for bein' there," he said. "Or bein' too old."

He picked up a stone and threw it. He'd been so still the movement startled me.

"She said no one wants a woman with a kid as old as me. She say that's why he lef'. She got mad and started cryin' and yellin' at me, worse than she ever did. If it weren't for me she coulda done somethin' with herself instead o' jus' me. She wouldn't o' been in this town or this job or this house. She'd have been better off weren't for me."

He leaned toward me and pointed at a small scar on his forehead. "That's where she got me. She slapped me first. I didn't do nothin'," he insisted, suddenly defensive. "I was so surprised. I jus' looked at her, like askin' 'why?' 'Why'd you hit me?' Then I could see it in her face. It got all screwed up while I was lookin' at her, like she woulda growled if she was a dog. It was like she was lookin' at all the things that was wrong. That's when she came at me. With her fists. Started slammin' at me over an' over." He mimicked flailing arms. "Like she wanted to cut me into little pieces. I backed up an' tried to hold her off but she kept comin'. Then I pushed her. I musta pushed hard 'cause she fell back and hit her head on the heater. It was so quiet all of a sudden. She'd been yellin' the whole time. Not words. Just sounds. Just..." he searched for the word, "mad."

He exhaled deeply and wrapped his arms, which he'd held aloft since miming his mother's rage, around his knees again.

"Was she hurt?" I asked.

"When she pulled her hand from the back of her head there was a little blood on her fingers, but that's all.

He was silent again.

"What'd she do?"

"Nothin'," he said. "She got up, slow. Didn't look at me the whole time. Walked real slow to her room and shut the door. Didn't see her 'til the next day when she got home from work, but she didn't say nothin' about it. Told me what she was leavin' me for dinner 'cause she was goin' to church that night.

He turned quickly to face me. "You ever go to church?" he asked and waited an earnest second. "Oh, yeah," he muttered, attention on the dirt once again, his disappointment palpable. "You said already."

He got very still and thoughtful for a moment, and then smiled and recited, "The Lord is coming out from his place to punish," he paused, trying to remember, "the inhabitants of earth for their iniquity." He stumbled on the last word. "And the earth will disclose the blood shed on it and will no more cover its slain."

His smile broadened when he was done. "I still remember that one," he boasted.

Louisa and Cindy sat down nearby in the dying, last light of day. The flashlight popped on, illuminating Cindy's book.

"Hey, come on," Jesse said, rising. "Let's go listen." He jogged toward them.

Did I get what I had wanted? Did he offer up his story, his life to me? I had prodded and he'd curled up like a pill bug and I'd poked some more and he'd spoken, finally, but I might as well not have bothered. I didn't feel I knew more than I had the hour before. I figured he didn't want anyone digging around inside and I wasn't that keen on it, either. He may have had something to hide. Frankly, I could sympathize, so I honored it. I didn't want anyone digging around either. He was his island, and I would be mine.

I followed Jesse. He scooted over so I could sit by him. By the flashlight, Louisa read from Cindy's storybook. The cacophony of stars, now endless up above, we huddled around the one small light. In the late dusk, Louisa and Cindy looked eerily beautiful with the light reflecting off the book's pages and onto their soft faces. Everyone else sat barely illumined, ghostly and still. Before she began, Louisa cast an eye across her audience, reeling us in. When she spoke, her voice was low, with nothing cloying or sentimental in it. In fact, her voice bore a jagged, wearied edge, presaging the story's end. "Once there was a tree and she loved a little boy," the tale began… The tree loved the boy so much she let the boy eat her fruit and sit in her shade, climb her trunk and swing from her branches. The boy loved the tree in return, the story went. But when the boy grew older, he often left the tree alone, and the tree grew lonely and sad. When the boy grew older still, he needed something more; so he asked the tree. He asked the tree for a boat so he could sail away. The tree loved the boy so much more than she loved herself, she allowed the boy to saw her down to make a boat and sail away, leaving what used to be a beautiful tree reduced to a bare stump, all alone. Years later, the boy returns, an old man now. The tree apologizes that she has no limbs for him to climb or fruit for him to eat, and the boy replies that he is too old to climb and has no teeth left with which to chew. He just needs a quiet place to sit and rest. It is the only thing the tree has left to offer him. The old man sits on the stump to rest, and the tree is happy. It was a sweet and brutal tale of love and giving, unforgiving age and loss.

Jesse blinked furiously, trying not to cry. Cindy leaned her head against Louisa. Night fell.

Later that night, as Jesse and Cindy were getting ready to sleep, I stood staring at the endless riot of stars and wondering where Paul had gone. Louisa approached and slipped her arm through mine.

"God, it's dark," she said.

"It's called nighttime."

"No moon, asshole." She smiled. "When I was thirteen or so, I went out into the woods—the real woods—for the first time. I saw my shadow and kept looking for the street lamps. I thought moonlight was something bad songwriters made up."

"You are *not* a country girl."

"Can't cook, don't sew, can't milk the cow." She stood silent for a moment. "But I'm pretty," she said. "And I'm real nice."

It was like a pressure on my chest. I breathed deeply as if to loosen it. Sensing my discomfort, she removed her arm from mine. I stared at the stars. I couldn't look at her. The pressure to care paralyzed me. It meant holding a thing as precious and dear to me and I was too scared to do that, too scared of losing it—whatever it was—although I couldn't even name it and it wasn't even mine.

"Oh, the look of terror on your face." She chuckled. "Don't worry," she continued, "I don't want you back. Though, if you ever grow up—and survive—you might be worth having."

The best I could do was to pat her hand as she turned to walk back toward the fire.

"I better go look for Paul," I said. Feeling the insufficiency of my response, I added, as if in penance, "Jesse won't bother you."

"I know," she replied.

Driving again, I was glad to be alone. Paul, Louisa, Cindy, Jesse, they all seemed like heavy branches dangling from me. I felt like they wanted something that I couldn't give but felt compelled to offer. In some ways, that was true, but I had wants as well. I couldn't conjure what would satisfy any of us—them, or me. I couldn't do it. I hadn't the will, the power, strength… I didn't have it. I wanted to scream at my impotence. I longed to disown all responsibility toward them and myself. 'This,' I thought, 'was supposed to be about something unidentifiably, yet tangibly larger than me—abstracts—about the world, eternity, living, the land.' I wondered when I, and all of these other mere people, had taken center stage.

Now I drove. Yet another escape.

VI

With only headlights and moonlight to guide me, I headed south, turned left or right on whims, driving on roads that barely qualified as such. After thirty minutes, I wasn't even sure what state I was in. Headlights punched little white holes in the dark, barely denting the pitch black western night. I was lost. I knew that and figured I'd have to wait until daylight to find my way back. There would be no retracing steps now. I planned to find a safe place to park and sleep in the car.

Then I saw the lights. Distant, they twinkled, like colorful, earthbound stars. As I got closer, the colors brightened—primaries, blue, green, red. They looked like Christmas lights. I headed for them. What the hell? Any suggestion of festivity would be an improvement. Soon, my high beams outlined a truck with the twinkling lights trailing it. Behind the truck, a travel trailer. An awning jutted from its roof, lined with the flashing lights I'd glimpsed in the dark a quarter mile back. A light shone from inside the trailer. Somebody home. Intrigued, I stopped. It was hard to imagine I'd be intruding; you don't festoon yourself with twinkling lights to warn folks off. But nonetheless, or for that very reason, I was a bit taken aback, maybe scared. I'd seen enough horror movies to fear strange trailers in the middle of nowhere dangling lights to lure you in. My car engine idled. Nothing stirred. No one. This wasn't even a real campsite. But I couldn't hold that against them. Yesterday I had found an equally illegitimate place to stake my tent. Maybe this was a kindred soul. Of course, in that case, I should have run. The last thing I needed was an addition to our crazy caravan.

The trailer door opened, but no one stepped out. I couldn't see anything inside, either. I waited a moment, but the door just hung there. In a similarly tentative gesture, I killed my engine. Total silence fell. It made these various metal vehicles seem all the more alien out here, staring silently at one another.

In for a penny, in for a pound, so I swung my leg out and set my left foot on the dusty ground. In response, the trailer door swung open a little wider. I swung the other foot out. Now both feet sat outside the car. The door did not respond in kind, so I stood. After a moment, she appeared. Not what I expected.

At first I only saw the outline, a nice figure, not plump, not thin, in a plain, light-colored dress gathered at the waist. As she stepped into the light, I saw that she was black—and I was shocked. I had barely seen any black people since I'd left the city. I tried to think how long it had been, but I couldn't. They'd pretty much disappeared. As I found the backroads and small towns that fed my romantic visions, they disappeared. I did not consider what that said about the idealized America that I'd been assured awaited me—the one I dreamed might rescue me. I didn't consider, at the time, what its whiteness meant.

She flicked an outside light on, illuminating both of us. She looked wary, as if deciding if she needed to prepare for battle. The corner of my mouth twitched in a pathetic attempt at a smile. She must have sensed that my nervousness matched hers. Her face relaxed and grew more curious than wary.

"What are you doing out here?" she asked.

"Nothing," I replied. "I was just driving… saw the lights."

She smiled as she looked up at the twinkling display. "I forget to turn these off."

She stepped outside the doorway. Her look grew mischievous. "Come on," she said. "I won't bite."

I took a few steps forward. She looked me up and down.

"I could tell you were a kid the minute you stepped out. Thought maybe you mistook me for one, too. I was startin' to get all flattered."

I blushed, and then blushed at the fact that I blushed.

"I'm Janice," she said.

"Lennie."

Closer, I couldn't tell her age. She might have been thirty, she might have been forty, but something in her mien made me think the latter. She was pretty and remarkably neat. Her light, patterned dress was perfectly pressed. She wore some makeup, not much, but it looked perfect. Her black hair was short and cut and curled like a perfectly sculptured little helmet. She looked both hard and kind.

"What are you doin' out here?" she asked again. "This place is nowhere on the way to nowhere else."

"It is. Just driving."

"Aimless driving down rough roads. Sounds serious."

"It's America." I smiled.

Her mouth moved as if to smile but she bit her lip, holding it back.

"Where do you come from?" she asked.

I was a little in awe. She seemed so real, so there, so sure of those two facts—her realness and her thereness—both so lacking in me. So I tried some bravado.

"Come on. Where you from?" she repeated.

"Nowhere," I replied, attempting worldliness. "All over."

This time she laughed. I couldn't tell if it was at or with me.

"You musta been born somewhere," she said.

"In the east."

"And raised?"

"In the east."

"All over," she mimicked without malice. "Nowhere."

"I meant," I sputtered desperately, "that I've never lived in one place since I've been grown."

"How long you been grown?" It dripped incredulity.

"I'm a musician," I spouted, astonished at my own lie. "A sax player. I go all over."

"A Travelin' Man," she dubbed me, laughing, and again I couldn't tell if I was the source or the object. "I've met some o' them before," she said with amused derision.

"What about you?" I asked, anxious to get the focus off of me.

"Me? I live here." She knocked the trailer.

"Not in this spot, I hope."

"No," she assured. "Just stopped here. Like you, found an out of the way place."

"There's a state park not far. It's off the main road."

She shook her head. "No. Don't like a lot of people. Not white folks. Not out here." I jerked back on 'white folks' as if she'd thrown something at me. It broke the rules. I was white, and this black woman said 'white folks' to me with fear and derision. I felt hurt. Then I didn't know if I should feel flattered that she didn't lump me in with 'them,' and then I felt resentful at the implication of the serious flaws my skin signaled to her. A whole ugly history leaped up at me, and she had roused it. In my eyes, she gained power for that moment; she glowed with it, and I wondered why more blacks didn't sling it in our faces every day to gain the upper hand I'd been taught all my life everyone ought to seek. I wondered what's the upside of black folks seeming so forgiving about their past, too much of their present, and the part white people played in it. Why wasn't I constantly reminded of my congenital role in that twisted inheritance? That I wasn't, that I was allowed to forget… it lessened them all in my eyes. It told me that she and her kind were of little consequence. She stood there, black, a jumble of power and impotence.

"I haven't seen a lot of black people out here." Again, it seemed wrong to say the word 'black' before a black person. It made me uncomfortable, but I forged on, assuming I was proving my worthiness—that I was not one of *them*.

"There ain't," she said. "Not out here." She made an expansive gesture. "I've never been out this way before," she said, indicating the land all around us. "I'm just seeing what there is to be seen. Wondering if any of it'll change anything."

"I don't know what you mean." I wanted to ask what needed changing, but I didn't dare.

"No matter," she said.

She switched gears entirely. Her face lit up and that mischievous glint returned. "Where you been, Travelin' Man? You been to other countries?"

I nodded.

"I wanted to go places when I was a girl, before..." she stopped herself. "Never did, though."

"You know," I said, "I thought you were a kid, too, from over there... your dress, the outline."

"Thought you were gonna get lucky, huh? No. It's just me, and I ain't no kid." She turned to look at her reflection in the glass of the trailer door. "I ain't no kid no more."

She turned to me and lit up again. She ran inside the trailer, then stuck her head out. "Come here," she insisted, bright as a child.

I looked inside the darkened box. One lone light shone in a far corner. I only saw outlines of furniture. And then horns blared and a rainbow of lights flashed as a jukebox lit up and whirred out a song I was thrilled to recognize: a bold, brassy blues, Dinah Washington again, whose "This Bitter Earth" Louisa and I had danced to on graduation day.

"I know this," I practically squealed as she stepped back outside.

My joy magnified hers and, like Louisa, she danced at me, daring me. I hesitated. She cocked her head in a 'shame on you' style. Embarrassed, I walked toward her. She grabbed my hand and twirled herself around, forcing me to move with her. Her glee was infectious. Blue, green, and yellow jukebox lights cast a deep technicolor glow outside the door. The dots of light circled and stuck to us like moths as we swooped and sashayed to that song's irresistible swing.

As the song ended, she laughed, catching her breath, and said, "You might not be so full of shit, Travelin' Man." She walked back inside the trailer. When she didn't come out again, I stuck my head in. She had lit a small lamp that barely touched the dark inside, but the jukebox still glowed. She turned it down as another song played. She stood at the sink, pouring herself a drink.

"You want one?" she asked.

"Sure."

"What?"

"Whatever you got."

"I got everything."

"Bourbon, then."

I stepped inside. It was small, but not as cramped as I would have thought. I'd never been in one before. I'd only seen them in movies and on TV. I sat on one of the bench seats on either side of the kitchen table. She brought the bottle and my drink and sank down on the other bench.

"I haven't danced like that in a long time. Thank you," she said as she lifted her glass. I lifted mine and we drank.

She leaned her head back against the wall. I realized that this might not have been her first drink of the evening.

"What you doin' out here, Travelin' Man?" Only this time, head back, eyes closed, she asked with an exhausted knowing, kneecapping my lies before I had time to mouth them.

"I don't know," I replied.

"Yes you do."

We sat, silent. The jukebox lights skittered across the darkened room.

"What are you doing here?" I asked in return.

"Hiding," she said, smiling.

"From what?"

She thought a moment and shrugged. "People. The past." She opened her eyes and looked at me, and I saw a bit of hatred there. "Maybe people like you," she added. "From John Reese," she said.

I didn't want to ask, but I had to. Not to ask would have been cowardly and an insult to this woman about whom I knew nothing, but whose respect I wanted—whose opinion mattered to me for reasons I didn't know.

"Who is he?"

"A dead man," she sighed. Then she looked me in the eye. "Don't you worry. Just one more dead nigger." The word was a slap and a challenge. She looked to see if I could meet it. When her eyes left mine I was sure I hadn't, so I asked. "Who was John Reese?"

She finished her drink and poured herself another.

"It's not your fight, boy. I shouldn't have said that."

"I want to know who he was," I persisted. "Tell me."

"You really do?" she asked, again as if daring me.

I nodded.

She cocked her head in a 'what the hell' gesture, leaned over and grabbed the bottle, and slid it closer to her. "They killed him," she said, matter of fact.

"Who?"

"All of 'em. Twenty-three years ago. Texas, twenty-three years ago." She finished off another drink. She poured herself yet another.

"You ever been to Texas?" she asked, still pouring.

I shook my head.

"The jukebox was like that one I got here. Nothin' special about the place. We hung out there, is all. It was our place. It was safe like that. I was about to graduate, and Leda and I used to go there almost every day. It's where I first heard Sarah Vaughan. Where I learned to dance with a boy.

"He was sixteen years old. Nice boy. Not the handsomest or anything. I was dancin' with him 'cause he asked. I was eighteen, and once we started, I was kinda teaching him. Felt sorry for him. Boy couldn't dance worth shit. I remember I was gettin' pissed at him 'cause he just could not move." She shook her head in amused dismay. "Then I heard it, like firecrackers, bam! bam! bam! bam! on and on like it wouldn't ever stop. The window glass cracked, loud, like two-by-fours smacking together. It scared us. We stopped and looked. And with my arms still around him, I saw from the corner of my eye 'cause I was looking at the window—his head just exploded. Pieces of it hit my face so hard it hurt, like someone beatin' me with a whip of John Reese's blood and brain."

She stopped, her mouth agape in wonderment. I didn't imagine she told this story often.

"Blood spattered all over my face. I had little bloody pieces of his head on my face and on my dress. He dropped to the ground, right outta my arms, like he shrank and melted. Then I heard more shots and saw two girls fall, and their blood. I stood there lookin' at them, my hands on my face trying to cover my eyes but never seeming to. I didn't do anything to help 'em. I couldn't move." She wiped her face. "I didn't scream or cry. I trembled like it was freezing cold.

"I wasn't no Pollyanna. I grew up there and I knew what white folks were." She leaned her head sideways, as if she couldn't, to this day, fathom her own shock. "I knew what they could do. I grew up with 'em callin' me 'nigger' and threatening to do shit like they did to everyone else colored in Texas. But this was different. They blew his brains out." She said the last like a plea, begging me to understand. She snapped her fingers to mark the suddenness. "On their whim, his head exploded like a little bomb.

"The two girls on the ground were rollin' around, screaming. Everyone was screaming. Some ran outside to try to see who did it. I saw it all, but I didn't move. Someone came over to me. She saw the blood on my face and thought I was shot, but I wasn't. She tried to pull my hands down from my face, but she couldn't. I tried to move. I was dancing with a sixteen-year-old boy to a tune on the juke and I heard a sound and his head... shattered and I was soaked in his blood. It was warm, almost hot on my face."

She poured more bourbon. Her hand shook. "Who can do that? Who has that power, a boy's head, an inch from yours, to make it explode like that?"

"Did they find who did it?" I asked.

She grinned. "Yeah. Twenty-two-year-old. Didn't want white folks to have to go to school with us. That was why he killed John Reese, tried to kill us all. They caught him. Even put him on trial. Found him guilty and set him free."

"How?" I asked.

"'Without malice,' they said. Said he did it 'without malice.' He blew John Reese's brains all over me without malice. How do you do that? You squash a bug without malice. That's how you swat a fly. How do you load a gun, get in a pickup truck, drive across to the black part of town, point that gun at black faces and pull the trigger again and again and again... *without malice*? When they said that, I stood there shaking." She held up her shaking hand. "I never really stopped."

I didn't want to ask any more questions.

"When the sentence came," she continued, "I broke down. I cried and cried. Everyone told me I had to move on. That's what colored folks did, they said. We move on. So I graduated from high school right there in Longview, Texas, looking every day at the same people who blew John Reese's blood and brains all over me. I tried not to be scared. Learned not to show it. But they weren't like me. They weren't human like me. They were something else. They could go on a joy ride and pop a black boy's skull like a blood-filled balloon. I wanted to cut one up like an autopsy to see what was inside, to see what the difference was."

"You got away," I said, as if doing her a favor by pointing out her personal triumph over adversity.

"I got married, and we moved to Atlanta. He was older than me. Felt safer that way. Never had any kids. Couldn't. Wouldn't. Not here, not with them—white—out there."

Her look left no doubt that I was one. I marveled that I didn't feel more ashamed.

"My husband died three years ago, and I've been out here ever since. Bought this rig and now I watch them. Like insects. From one end of this country to the other. First place I went was Longview, Texas. Couldn't stay long, though. Couldn't walk down the street with every other step an American flag slapping me in the face like it was supposed to mean somethin'.

"I don't live here anymore. I live… above this country, around it. I keep moving."

"I'm sorry," I said.

"Don't flatter yourself, boy. Would you have been any different? With your Mama and Daddy tellin' you what filth I was and how much better you were than me, would you have been different?" She shook her head. "You're just as white and you would've stood up and cheered in that courtroom right alongside the rest of 'em."

I wanted to defend myself and demand that I would have been among the few, but I couldn't. I couldn't be sure. That's what silenced me. There was a murderer in most of the faces she saw each day. Supposedly innocent faces, driving down the street, in stores, on playgrounds… faces like mine.

"What you doin' out here, Travelin' Man?" she repeated, her small smile genuine now, and hinting of kindness and sympathy. Perhaps she saw that I wanted to be something better, even if I couldn't promise that I was.

I returned the smile. "Oh… I'm just tryin' to learn…" I scoffed at the thought but decided to go for it, 'how to fly,' I half-kidded, remembering Becca's graduation goodbye.

"I learned a story once," she replied, "about a special boy who wanted to fly. You know it?" she asked.

I shrugged, curious.

"He made pretty wings out of wax and feathers," she said, "and then flew too close to the sun."

"I know that one," I smiled, "but I don't think I'm special."

"Yes, you do," she replied, eyeing me. I felt embarrassed.

Finally, she released me and leaned her head back against the wall once more and closed her eyes.

I stood to leave. She didn't protest. "It's too bad you ain't older, and I ain't younger," she said. "You ain't blacker and I ain't whiter. We might have got along."

I looked at her as I stood in the doorway, her eyes closed, head leaned back, fury and resistance on her face.

"You ain't no musician," she whispered, her eyes half closed. "And you ain't no Travelin' Man."

I stepped out into the night. The desert floor was like a different planet after my time inside with her. I sat in my car, looking at the trailer plopped there, like a porthole to an alternate place where time slowed and the past walked. As I watched, the flashing, multi-colored lights went dark. The trailer disappeared until I fired up the car and the headlights hit it. As I veered away, it disappeared again.

She had no business being there. I never found the place again. God knows I tried. Over time, I spent weeks driving every road I could find in northeast Arizona, southeast Utah, and even northwest New Mexico, but I couldn't find her. Eventually, I questioned if she'd really been there. Could I have been truly mad to do what I'd done… run away, drag others with me, scoop up strays like an accidental net way out in the nether-reaches of a country I barely knew? It would be nice to believe that I dreamed it all, but I'm reminded daily that at least some of it was real.

PART II

VII

Ten years later—about ten years ago—something changed. I would become aware of sitting, doing nothing, and then I'd realize I'd been reliving those days. Thrown back in time, I'd find myself in that car, Jesse's face in the rearview mirror. The past crept in on me.

Until then, I had disappeared. I took jobs that I didn't need and didn't care about in order to have something to do. For several years, I became someone else. My backstory changed. I was born and raised in Pennsylvania to hard-working parents who still lived there. It's amazing how thoroughly you can mask your life to the point where you don't even notice the rubber band anymore. Not until it snaps. I walked through the workdays, laughed through lunches, shared drinks with coworkers at the odd happy hour, all as someone else. Home alone, I became no one—not myself certainly, and no longer the masked man who walked the daylight hours. Alone, I entered a kind of netherworld, a bubble of my own that omitted the past and ignored the present until it was time to don the mask again and put on another show.

But the band did snap and the mask slipped. A TV in a workplace break room flashed "Special Report" and news helicopter footage of a high-speed car chase took over the screen. The car weaved raggedly through traffic until police cars bottled it up in a cul-de-sac. Then all the cars just sat there—the police cars and the car being chased. I watched as the TV sound went black in my ears. My hand shook, and then my arm, and my leg, and I fell. I tried to get up, but I couldn't. My limbs were too weak. People rushed over to help and I tried to wave them off but was so obviously incapacitated that they called an ambulance. By the time I got to the hospital, I had pretty much recovered. I only felt some lingering weakness. They wanted to do tests, but I declined. I knew what had happened. The band had snapped; and I knew immediately that I couldn't hide from what happened anymore—at least not like this.

I was drawn west again, back to where it happened. I had to go. I took apartments a few months at a time here and there and finally settled in New Mexico, outside Santa Fe. That was a first step, the landscape reminding me, always whispering something just out of earshot, something important, something I didn't dare strain to hear. It grew louder over time, until I couldn't deny it anymore. "*Look at what you've done,*" it said. And then the images came, but they seemed like something from a movie I'd half forgotten.

"*Look at what you've done.*"

I couldn't tell if it was a voice of pride or horror. I wanted to shout back that I had done nothing. Nothing!

The sound and the images, the landscape all around me testifying to the permanence of what had happened during those days on the road… There was no more hiding. I had to return to it, and I tried, but the results were confused and only unsettled me more.

It's like I woke up after ten years. Running as far and as fast as I could, I'd relegated all of it to the realm of magic and the Fates. No choices, no blame, no right, no wrong. To me, over the years, the whole episode had become chimerical. Less than real, it had no cause and no consequences. It could be safely stored and forgotten; and I could be someone it had never touched. Now, it crept fully back—the real, the flesh and the blood, and I had spent so long embellishing it with fateful fancies in order to absolve myself of… everything, that I didn't even know what was real anymore. I didn't know how much of my recollection I could trust, and how much was wishful dreamings I'd woven to tempt myself to forget. The problem with blaming everything on the fates is that you're reduced to a pawn. And in my case, a pawn that's cursed, downright damned to be and deserve nothing more than what I found out in the desert in my quest for… I didn't even know anymore.

Unable to trust myself, I had to rebuild it, action by action, point-of-view by point-of-view, so I could lay it out like a puzzle or a skeleton and glimpse the whole. I had to know what I had done. That whole, in its completeness, would assure me that I was not cursed or damned, but simply a fool, or unlucky, that those events made some kind of sense when you put them all together, that they didn't spring from the malicious intents of the gods. That it was over and I needn't be scared anymore—that I might have a life that both absorbed it and left it behind.

I began another trek. I started looking back at what I had so brilliantly... diminished. For ten years I had wandered, concealing the existence of those few days. Doing so, keeping the memories at bay, that was my vocation, and it left little room for anything else. But the strength of my weakness failed me. The flames rose and I couldn't tamp them down. I felt the heat of the memories.

After my collapse, I rattled the bars of the cage my denial had created. My refusal to regard that time, my insistence on averting my gaze, it had left those events to live as myth or dream, and to dominate me completely. My backstory had changed, but I had not. Through denial, I had stayed the same romantic fatalist I'd been right out of college. I'd stayed too much the same boy I'd been back then.

So, for the first time in almost ten years, I sought the others out—the characters from my storied journey. Sadly, after it happened, I had only minor communications with Louisa, and only for a while. I had tried to keep in touch, but I couldn't. It hurt too much to remember, and her voice, her handwriting; it all reminded me. She reached out, and called and wrote, but I kept my distance, and she finally gave up, to my relief. As with Louisa, I had tried to keep in touch with Paul soon after, but he never responded, and I quickly abandoned my attempts.

Now there were things I had to know—the next step in the never-ending process that those senseless incidents had become. I tracked down almost everyone. I meant to interrogate each of them and put the whole thing back together, from every point of view, so I could stare at it—the whole all neatly laid out—and finally call it finished. I started with those about whom I knew the least, the first of whom was Mrs. Gerald, Cindy's mother.

She wasn't hard to locate. No one is unless they're trying to hide. Once I found her, I called. As I listened to the phone ringing, I thought she'd refuse to speak to me. From her viewpoint, I thought she'd have nothing to gain. But I underestimated how deep a bond you make with your wounds. She had hoarded enough anger and brittleness about the whole thing to want to air it, walk it, let it frolic for a while. I got the sense she was angry and brittle about a lot. After a few phone calls and a couple of semi-sadistic false alarms (her agreeing and then bailing at the last moment), I arrived at her door. That last time I got her to commit to a meeting, I didn't answer her calls. She didn't get the chance to back away.

I thought I'd dread the interview, but I surprised myself by looking forward to it—looking back at the damage done. It's like old home movies—the ones where colors turn vivid and burnt with time, the faces all grainy. In those, the memories seem more precious for the deterioration they've endured. It was like opening an old box of photos holding pictures that used to hurt too much to look at.

She lived in a mobile home park in Northern California—a fairly nice one with units adequately spaced among tall Ponderosa pines. I lived in New Mexico, so it wasn't that far. The town was small, about ten miles up the hill from a larger college town. I saw lots of seniors. The place had a big retirement contingent. Hurricane-fenced yards held everything from goats to rusted-out cars. Some were neat as pins. A little bit of everything. Working class. A fair amount of poor folks.

She answered the door with a cigarette in hand; I vaguely recalled her smoking in the restaurant ten years prior. She attempted a smile as she ushered me in. She looked the same—older, but still herself. Sometimes I'll see seniors and it's hard to imagine they're the same person as the young one in the photo on the wall. She seemed one of those people who would always look herself, regardless of age. I had always hoped to be one of those. It heartened me to see Mrs. Gerald managing it. I sat on a plaid sofa in a room tidy with discount furniture. It smelled of eggs.

"I remember your face," she said, a bit accusatory, as she slid into a large green lounger. She grabbed the remote and muted the TV. She noted my limp as I walked to a chair. She didn't ask about it and I didn't explain.

"I'm just glad my face is still recognizable," I tried to joke.

"I'll never forget." She scowled and nodded emphatically. "You people took my daughter."

I lowered my head. This, at least, I knew for certain. "We didn't know she was there, Mrs. Gerald. She snuck into the car."

With a pursed mouth she shook her head dismissively. "I saw you in the restaurant," she raised her voice a notch. "I saw you goading her. I remember to this day. I told that cop, and he acted like he didn't believe me."

I remained silent. It was obvious that the facts couldn't sway her. She had a lot invested in this version of the truth—just as I had had in avoidance.

I changed the subject. "Do you see much of Cindy?" I asked. "How is she?"

She leaned back. "She called, not long ago." She stamped out her cigarette, smoked down to the filter. "You know, me and her father got divorced soon after. I made damn sure she came to live with me." She paused, her expression churning as if digesting the hurt. "But you folks had done a number on her. She was never the same."

I wanted to ask how she'd changed, but I didn't dare. The answer could have been too painful.

"I'm trying to understand what happened," I said, remembering why I came, "after we left the restaurant—the order of events… when you realized she was missing, when the police got involved… what you saw."

She sighed and settled a little, preparing herself. She shrugged in 'why not' acquiescence and looked me in the eye for the first time. "She was gone too long. I noticed it. Hank, my husband at the time, he'd say he did, but it was me. I'm the one who went looking for her." She lit another cigarette. "She wasn't in the ladies' room, so I came out and looked around the restaurant. I was getting scared then… mad… she'd run off sometimes, drive me crazy… I motioned back to the table for

Hank to help me look. He didn't know what I was saying, so he came over and I told him I couldn't find her. He started askin' around. Finally someone said they saw her walk out the door, thought it was strange that she was alone."

She slapped at her eye. She didn't want me to see them welling up. I didn't want to make her feel worse, but dredging up the past is what I'd come to do.

"Why did she leave?"

She became motionless with fury as she looked at me. But then it passed, like a flush. She averted her eyes and didn't answer.

"When did the police come?"

Past the pride of hiding her tears, she pulled a tissue, wiped her nose, and quickly dabbed her eyes.

"We got more frantic and asked all the waitresses and half the customers. Someone called the police, I don't know who, but I remember someone saying they did. The manager sat with us. I was so mad. I wanted to hit Hank. I wanted to pound on him right there. We were there because of him. If he had done what any man ought to do we would've been somewhere else and she would have been safe. I wanted to hit him, but I cried instead. He was so scared he didn't say a word. Not a thing. He loved that girl like nothing else. That was the problem. Looking at him so scared made me madder. It's what all this was about."

"Where were you headed?"

She looked at me, clearly deciding if I deserved to know. In the end, it was more apparent that she needed to tell.

"A different life," she said. At the memory, she smiled, showing the first I'd seen of anything resembling hope or happiness. "Down to Dallas. Hank was in the Army. He joined when he was a kid, and I guess didn't think any more about it. When I met him he seemed happy, content. I was a little older than him, and I guess I liked that. I was good enough to get myself a younger man. Most women were married and had kids by the time me and him got together. He was different from me, so light, nothin' bothered him, not a worrier like me. I'd chew on somethin' until nothing was left and then worry about what I swallowed. He was nothing like that. Stuff just rolled off his back. Made me feel lighter when I was around him, and I liked that. I guess that's why it worked with him when it never did before. He was so different.

"I got pregnant with Cindy, and he asked me to marry him." She smiled at the memory. "I didn't expect that. A voice in my head kept sayin' that he'd run, and that I'd wind up alone. I thought it out. I knew how to get an abortion. I found out how, and if that happened, it was okay. I didn't... *not* want a child, but I wasn't one of those who wanted one really bad either. I don't know. I wasn't engaged, wasn't married. Now this was happening when it shouldn't have...

"But he surprised me and asked me to marry him. And it wasn't grudging or anything. When I said 'yes,' his face lit up and he smiled a mile wide. He grabbed me up in his arms harder than anyone ever had and kissed my eyes and my cheeks and my forehead again and again. He spun me around. I'd never seen anyone so happy. My mouth was wide open. I must've looked like a cartoon or something. Shocked. Just shocked. And then happy, and I was kissing him back and grabbing handfuls of his uniform like I'd never let go. I didn't think I ever would.

"After Cindy, Hank got family quarters on post. It wasn't bad, not for a start. That's what I thought. But then a year went by, and I asked him when we'd get a place. You know, buy something, off-base. He shrugged, like he never thought of it.

"Nothing changed. Not in two years. He loved Cindy and he was good to me, but nothing changed. I had an idea of doing more, moving up, you know. But he was fine on the base. Once Cindy was two years old or so, I started thinkin' about working again. I had been a receptionist in a dentist's office before I married. I quit that with Cindy, but I was thinking about using the military, maybe, goin' to school, a dental hygienist maybe. They made good money. I remember he was playing with Cindy, tossing her up in the air, helping her stay upright when she was learning how to run. I told him about wanting to go back to school. He didn't object, but without taking his eyes off Cindy, smilin' and playing with her, he said, 'Sure, but you don't need to. We got everything we need.'

"It was so matter-of-fact. I almost believed him for a minute. He had what he needed. That's what started it. That day. That's when I knew I had to get him needin' more. I didn't want to spend my life in Army housing on an Army base. I wanted to go somewhere else, maybe, somewhere better. Part of getting married was doin' that with someone—moving up. So I started talking to him about it, telling him that we owed it to Cindy to do better. That's right, isn't it? That's what you do."

It wasn't a rhetorical question but I didn't answer. She wanted reassurance. She wanted to know if she had aimed at the wrong star. I had no idea. She was a working class woman and I had no clue what such women wanted or were expected to do. I had always been rich, and because of that, I know, I inhabit a different world. Over the years and years of wealth, I've been changed, wired differently, fundamentally so, from most. I had nothing to offer her. I just knew that my mother, too, as wealthy as she was, had pushed a man, dangerously, to greater heights.

She saw that I wouldn't, or couldn't, offer more. She shrugged it off.

"Once I got that idea in my head, I couldn't shake it loose. The idea sat back there." She pointed at her head. "I'd talk about it now and then with Hank, but not that much. I thought it would happen, you know, spontaneously, with little hints. Almost by itself. I had to plant the seed, that's all.

"When Cindy started school, I went back myself, like I said. Got to be a dental hygienist. He didn't complain or say anything about it. Said he was happy if I was, but nothin' changed. He didn't take the hint. I started working part time, bringing in money, started fixing up the place, even got a new car. He seemed very pleased for me, but acted like the rest didn't matter. He kept on sayin', 'If you're happy, I am.'"

"But you weren't happy," I said.

"He wasn't going to make anything in the Army. He was NCO. Not unless he got college, and when I talked to him about that, he said it wasn't for him. And that was that. He was ready to stay right where he was. It was years I waited." She sat back in her chair. "I got mad.

"At that restaurant, we were on our way to Fort Worth. A girl I worked with had moved to Dallas. She had relations in the big phone company there. Said they could get him a job and that there'd be plenty of work for me. Of course, he said no, but I didn't let it go. I told him that he couldn't just keep us here, me and Cindy, keep us standing still. I kept telling him that he couldn't do that to her. This woman I knew worked in a good school in Dallas, private school. Said she could help us get Cindy in on a special program. When I told him it had boarding, too, he had a fit. Accused me of trying to give my daughter away. I guess I got to be the biggest bitch in the Midwest, but he didn't leave me any choice. What else was I gonna do? Leave me and my daughter to rot on some goddamned Army base?"

She reached for her cigarette, but it had burned out. She lit another. "It all broke loose on the road. First he kind of pleaded. Said that me and Cindy was all he wanted, the job was fine, and it was enough. He got pissed when I said men were supposed to do better for their families. He said a woman was supposed to raise her child and be home with it. That set me off 'cause he never said a word about me working. Not a word. It got worse from there. Finally he said that if I wanted something else, I better go get it. I said I would. That was that."

"Cindy heard this?"

"Probably. A lot of it. Her disappearing seemed like... just more of the fight."

"What happened when the police came?"

She waved her hand, dismissive. "They talked to everyone. They told us about you folks, about the gas station, and how you left the restaurant right after Cindy. I told 'em that you'd been talking to her. They figured you took her."

"We didn't. We didn't know she was in the car for hours."

"Why didn't you bring her back, call the police?"

"We were going to. That was the plan. It got strange. We were trying..."

She pursed her lips, contemptuous of excuses. We faded into silence again.

"How is Cindy?" I asked.

"She's grown. I don't see her much. She lived with me, right after. For five years. It was good for a while, but when she got a bit older, we fought. You know girls that age. She went to live with her father. Did you talk to him?"

"I asked, but he wouldn't. We spoke briefly on the phone, but that was all. He said there wasn't any reason."

She smiled, unamused. "Just like him. Let things lie. Standing still. Haven't seen him in… long time. She tells me he's okay. You seen her?"

"No," I replied, but I felt the need to make excuses. "She was with us. I know what she knew. There's really no reason to contact her."

"You could say you're sorry."

Perhaps it showed on my face—that I didn't talk to Cindy because I was too scared to face the damage I might have done.

"I am sorry," I said. "I am. But right now, I need to know what happened. I need to understand why."

"After all this time?"

"Yes."

She pinched her lips in incredulity. "It was only later that I found out that you were all rich kids. I guess that's why nothin' happened to you."

The word 'bitch' crossed my mind. She had seen my remorse with her own eyes, but still she dug the knife in. I resented her despite the fact she probably had the right.

"That's how you got away with takin' my daughter from me. She was never the same."

"Thank you." I stood. "For seeing me."

"Why didn't you just bring her back?" She asked with such frustration and regret, she might have asked why time had passed.

"We were trying." I said, exhaustedly. "We were."

VIII

I TOOK A CIRCUITOUS route back from Janice's brightly festooned, ghost-filled trailer. I drove for hours trying to get back to our campsite. It seemed so hopeless that I finally pulled off the road, killed the engine, and closed my eyes a while. I jerked awake about two hours later, daylight peeking in.

I looked around and recognized where I was. I quickly revved up the engine and a mere five minutes ahead, I saw a road sign I remembered; I had passed it the day before on the way to the campsite. I slapped the steering wheel with satisfaction. Relief and contentment rode shotgun all of a sudden. Last night receded like a reverie.

The sun crept over the desert, and I felt that something had changed—not only that I could find my way back. Jesse and his gun, Cindy's stowing away, the fight with Paul, my absurd outburst, and then the surreal night with the phantasmic woman in a caravan in the middle of nowhere who mourned dead boys and wandered through the grandiloquent hell that had murdered them—it made no sense. There was no neat English Lit cause-and-effect, no TV plot diagram, but they all added up to something that I felt right then. Inarticulable, it was outside of my resting place of logic and rationality. Like the events that produced it, the sense I had was knotty and web-like, not glossy, not sequential. A sense of resolution settled on me. It had appeared as suddenly as Jesse and Cindy, but there it was. A wave had crested and broken. I felt different, that's all. Rinsed free of whatever had driven me so hard. I was perfectly willing to stay, drive more, see more. But I no longer needed the world to sit up and howl because I did so. Perhaps an acknowledgment of my own romantic foolishness. Jesse was a scared boy, not my personal outlaw. Ten-year-old Cindy found her world so dangerous that she took a chance on strangers. Janice had been splattered with blood that might have been acid it had scarred so deeply. All worlds outside mine. Wandering American roads to await my proclamation as the center of all things seemed, now, as foolish and hopelessly young as it really was.

As I drove up to the campsite, Louisa greeted me.

"Hi," she said, exploratory, not knowing whom she'd find.

"Howdy. Everything all right?"

"Yeah. Paul got back last night. Still looked pissed. He ignored me; just jumped in his sleeping bag."

Big sigh. "Okay."

She stood waiting. "And…?" she asked. "Where've you been?"

"Took a drive," I replied, deciding how much to tell her. "I got lost and then found something… strange. Nevermind. I'll tell you later. I'm too tired. You get some sleep?"

"Yeah."

I tossed her the keys. "You drive."

"First business…"

"Cindy," I said, cutting her off. "I know."

She headed off to rouse the others. "Wakey wakey, rise and shine, kiddies!" she sang as she kicked prone bodies blanketed on the sand.

"It ain't barely light yet," Jesse complained.

I threw some things in the trunk. When I approached, Paul stood there with an armful of sleeping bag. Neither of us knew what to say.

"You okay?" I asked.

He nodded. Silence again. I watched Jesse pull his shoes on as Cindy folded up her blanket. Paul's eyes followed mine.

"Look," I said, trying to explain with a minimum of embarrassment, "I know he's just a fucked up kid and now we'll drop him somewhere and take Cindy to the cops and explain the whole thing. They'll get her back to her parents."

He nodded again, half satisfied but still resentful. As he walked away, he stopped and asked, "Where'd you go?"

"I found," I said, still not knowing how to explain without sounding ridiculous, "a ghost town… not far from here."

Practically hidden by the bedroll she carried, Cindy screamed at the top of her lungs, "I'm hungry!" I threw a sleeping bag over her head. She dropped her roll and spread her arms like a ghost, chasing blindly and giggling mightily. Paul even stifled a smile.

I felt good as we jumped in the car. Paul shocked me by climbing in the back seat. Granted, he tucked himself as deep into the corner as he could, but he was sharing the back with Jesse. It was a major gesture. Jesse gazed at me, open-mouthed but with a clear pleasure at this token of acceptance. Cindy kept pleading hunger, so food became first business. We stopped at the next fast food joint heralding breakfast items. Paul and I kept catching and avoiding each other's eyes in the rearview mirror as we sat in the drive-thru line. He and I obviously had some talking to do. The already-greasy white bags passed through the driver's side window and Louisa matched items to orderers.

Back on the freeway, we picked up speed.

"That was not a restaurant," Paul drawled as he spat half-chewed pabulum back into its Styrofoam carton. "It was a vomitorium." Cindy picked up a doughy disk and held it before her face as if it were a trapped butterfly, turning it this way and that with a field guide's concentration, before she slapped it against the back windshield, to which it stuck.

Each of us tossed a greasy fast-food bag into the trash bin outside the next diner we found—a small mom-and-pop place. We settled in a booth and ordered. Louisa pointed delightedly at the TV on a corner shelf as Bugs, Yosemite Sam, and the Road Runner marched across the screen. Her smile disappeared as the words "Special Report" both filled and silenced the TV. There were about ten other diners in the place. It had their attention as well.

A news anchor appeared, his hand on his earpiece as he absorbed instructions.

"We don't have all the details yet," he began, "but we have new details on the story we've been following about a gunman who held up a gas station near the Oklahoma border yesterday, and either abducted or was assisted by three other young people, two male, one female, all said to be in their early twenties. At least one wore a Harvard University T-shirt. Also yesterday, ten-year-old Cindy Gerald was reported missing from a local restaurant where the gunman and the young people had been seen. They left about the same time the girl disappeared."

Cindy's face filled the screen. Ridiculously, I looked at the girl across the table to verify the resemblance.

"Police are considering that the group may have kidnapped the girl."

Every eye in the place turned on us. It was surreal, like we were in two places at once—one on the TV and one in a diner trying to have some breakfast before we made all of this go away.

"Police… considered… asking the public… ten years old, four feet five inches… gunman… group armed… shoulder-length brown… call…"

I heard bits and pieces. We didn't know that the holdup and the gas station fireball had caused a sensation. We didn't know that spectacular photos of the gas-fueled conflagration played in endless rotation on every local channel. The cops had responded with corresponding zeal. Our fellow diners found themselves in the midst of a sensation.

Smack in the middle of the diner, a middle-aged man stood up slowly. Eyes glued to our booth, he backed toward the door. Other patrons looked fretfully left and right, as if checking for accomplices. Another stood, a woman this time. She scurried to the door, hunched down and curled into herself like she desperately had to pee. A crash as a chair fell backwards and another man ran for his life. And then mayhem as seats shot out from under patrons dashing for the exits. Cars revved and squealed from the parking lot. They looked so scared. I tried to make my face beam, "Wait. It's a mistake. We're harmless." My hand actually patted the air as if to soothe them.

Like a needle plopped mid-record, Daffy and Donald marched across the TV screen again. "On with the show, this is iiit…"

"Was it something I said?" Paul announced to the now-empty room.

"Come on."

I jumped from the table and race-walked to the car. By the jumblings and rustlings behind, I knew everyone was following. The engine thundered. The doors slammed and tires whined as we sped from the parking lot.

Paul, Louisa, and Jesse kept looking through the back windshield to see if anybody followed us. Cindy climbed into the back between Paul and Jesse so she could get a better view. Nobody spoke for a good mile. I wasn't scared. I was indignant. The idea that we had helped Jesse rob a gas station was grotesque. The notion that we had kidnapped Cindy even more so. They… "They," the great "they" out there… they were looking at us through twisted eyes. Their vision had to be righted. That was my thought. No one had ever thought of me, of any of us, in those terms before—as criminals, for God's sake—never as anything other than the elect. No one had ever doubted my veracity or failed to acknowledge my access to the benefit of the doubt.

"Kidnapped!" Paul finally blubbered. "Do you believe that?"

"Why don' we just tell 'em she wanted to come?" Jesse asked.

"We will. This kidnapping thing is ridiculous."

"But that doesn't do away with the robbery," Paul added, nodding toward Jesse.

"How much did you get from that?" I asked, wondering what level of seriousness we dealt with.

Jesse dug into his pant pocket and pulled out some bills and change. He counted.

"Bout five bucks… and some change here…"

Paul's jaw dropped. "Five bucks!"

"That's all the guy had on him," Jesse said, defensive.

"Jesus Christ!" Louisa slumped down in the passenger seat.

"All this for five bucks," Paul kept shaking his head.

I actually turned from the road to face Jesse. "So you didn't have any bullets, and you took all of five bucks?"

Paul's palms flew skyward in disbelief. A few staccato exhalations then a full-throated guffaw.

"No bullets… gun wasn't…" He couldn't talk for simultaneously swallowing astonishment and laughing. I looked at Louisa, accusatory.

I just assumed she had told Paul about the gun. She shrugged peevishly in a 'what are you looking at me for' gesture.

"And you thought," Paul blurted, pointing at me, "you thought we were on the run with one of the Dillinger gang!" He fell backwards laughing, knees up and arms across the belly.

"You mean," I turned and said to Jesse, dealing with the new surprise, "you only robbed the clerk? Why didn't you hit the cash register?"

"I didn't have time," he shouted.

Paul kicked the back of the front seat like a furious cyclist while his laughter filled the car. Cindy giggled, unsure why. Louisa chuckled as Paul's kicks rattled her brains. I turned back to the road, head slowly shaking.

"What's so funny?" giggling Cindy finally asked.

"Looks like the laugh's on you this time, bucko!" Paul said, poking his finger in my back.

"All right, all right," I conceded.

"I never thought of you," he added, his laughter fading, "as a gag man before."

It was hard to imagine that I had whispered "life and death," in Paul's ear the night before. Hard to believe that I had somehow concocted this caravan-of-the-absurd in a grandiose bid to converse with no lesser entity than Providence. I smiled at the thought that I was ridiculous. I didn't mourn the former self that would have railed at the idea.

Looking at the road ahead, I knew I had to find the nearest town. I'd drive to the police station and calmly herd everyone inside. I would explain. That would be the end of it. I didn't know what would happen to Jesse. I checked him in the rearview mirror. He sulked in the corner, arms tight across his chest. He must have thought we were laughing at him. I planned to pull over before we stopped and talk to him.

Cindy spotted it first. She was staring skyward. I saw her in the rearview mirror and at first, I didn't pay any attention, but she kept looking up. Then I heard thumping, growing louder and louder until it was deafening, and the sound didn't pass. It stayed, like a raging, thunderous heartbeat. In my side mirror, right behind us, I saw the police helicopter.

"Folks," I heard myself say, "I think this is it."

"Look." Louisa pointed ahead. Police cars flanked both sides of the road. Cops on the far sides stared through binoculars. I slowed down. Red and blue lights flashed from the cop car roofs.

"What are they doing?"

Fear in Louisa's voice. My heart pounded. As we approached, I saw their rifles. I slowed down again. I checked the speedometer. I was driving 20. I didn't know if I should stop. They weren't in front of us or blocking the road. I slowed down some more.

"What do we do?" Louisa asked, panic growing. The helicopter thwapped overhead.

"Cindy…" I said.

"I know," she replied. "They're gonna take me back."

"'Fraid so, hon," Louisa said.

"What are they gonna do to me?" Jesse cried.

"It can't be much," I said. "You didn't do anything. We'll talk to 'em first."

"What are we doing now?" Paul demanded.

"I don't know. I can't stop. I don't wanna stop 'til they tell me to."

"We gotta talk to 'em.".

"That's what I just said."

"Where, then?"

"I don't know where!"

The police waited a few yards ahead. The helicopter hovered closest to the driver side. Its noise still slapped my eardrums.

I barely heard the siren with the deafening thwack so close it seemed to suck the air right out of the car. A flashing light sped toward us from behind. I realized there were no other cars on the road.

Jesse: "We gotta get to California."

The helicopter noise might as well have disappeared. He didn't sound angry or panicked. He was calm, but his tone commanded all of our attention.

"I never seen the ocean. You said we were goin'."

"We were," I said.

We approached the cop cars on either side of the road. I didn't dare stop; I didn't know what they wanted me to do. Still creeping along, I drove. I passed them. Still no instruction. In the mirrors, I saw the cops jump in and follow, red lights flashing.

"I'll go," Paul blurted. "I'll talk to 'em… and tell 'em."

No one responded.

"Let me out," Paul said.

Jesse: "No."

I couldn't read him. I couldn't read his face. He didn't look angry. He looked blank. "Jesse?"

"I never did nothin' to you!" he shouted at Paul.

"Cindy," Louisa reached out to the girl. "Why don't you climb up here with me?"

After a moment of looking from Paul to Jesse to see if it was safe, she did.

"How much further we got?" Jesse asked.

Paul: "What?"

"'Til we get to California."

"Don't you understand!?" Paul screamed.

"It's a long way, Jesse." I tried to sound calm. "We've got a third of the country to cross."

"How long's it gonna take?"

"It would take days," I replied.

He thought for a moment. "That's all right," he said.

"Look out the window!" Paul yelled. "You think they'll just follow us 'til we get there?"

Jesse railed, "You said they wasn't gonna kill me for takin' five bucks!" Tears ran down his face.

"No one's gonna kill anyone!" I shouted, terrified at the talk of killing.

Louisa whispered, "Lennie, why don't you just let Cindy out for now?" She turned to Jesse, her voice low and calm. "Then we can keep going. I think they just want Cindy back."

"She said she don't wanna go."

"That's all right," Cindy smiled. "I don't mind."

"Hey, kid… I thought you and me was gonna race to the ocean."

"I don't wanna cause more trouble." Seeing the sadness on his face she added, "Maybe I'll meet you there."

An unmarked car approached from behind. It caught up with us and sped past on the right. I saw two men and a woman inside. I thought I recognized the woman. Cindy, on Louisa's lap, watched them pass. Sadness swept over her.

"Not her," she muttered.

Louisa laid her head on Cindy's shoulder and closed her eyes against tears. The passing car carried Cindy's parents.

"They'd kill us if she left," Jesse repeated as the car sped by, as certain as he was of solid ground below us.

"They're not gonna kill anybody!" Paul insisted with the desperation of someone battling an insane idea for fear it might take hold.

"What are they doing?" Louisa pointed as one police car slowed and came parallel with ours. Jesse threw himself against the back seat. Paul jumped away. Jesse's arm jutted out. I glimpsed the gun in the rearview mirror.

The first shot sucked the air from the car. Glass exploded. I heard screams. I instinctively ducked and the car swerved wildly. Another shot thundered like hammer on anvil and my foot flattened on the gas. I couldn't see. I lifted my head as I sped past blood splattered like magenta paint on the spider web cracks of the police car windows.

It was hard to hear. Just ringing. Screams. Some were mine. I opened my eyes. I stomped on the brakes when the car flew off the road and danced on the shoulder.

"Drive! Drive!" Jesse shouted. He pointed the gun at my head. I saw his face, a mask of fury and terror. "DRIVE!" he shrieked.

I stomped on the gas. Jesse panting like trapped prey, huddled in the corner, pointing the gun at all of us. The screams quieted as the car zoomed ahead. Police cars swerved onto the road behind us, sirens blaring. Cindy whimpered and Louisa tried to quiet her. Paul wiped the tears from his face.

The car's big engine roared. I barely heard the helicopter hovering high above. The world shrank to a narrow metal corridor lined with guns and dotted with blood. I saw the blood again and again. There was so much of it. I told myself that it was an illusion, that it wasn't that bad, that the paint splatter of blood inside the car windows was nothing more than a vision born of fear.

I saw movement up ahead. Jesse leaned forward to look. Police cars blocked the road. More cars sat on the side. Outside each stood men with guns.

I slowed. I tried to do it so gradually that no one in the car would get alarmed, and I don't think they did. Every second the police cars and guns got closer. As we approached, they took aim at the car.

I swerved and drove off the road. There were audible gasps as the car lurched and undulated recklessly across the landscape and up a small slope from the road. I drove a good quarter mile and then stopped and killed the engine. I was sweating. I don't know why I drove off the road, but I did it. Maybe there was nothing else to do.

"Whatchu stoppin' here for?" Jesse demanded.

"We can't drive on this," I hissed, surprising myself with the impatient tone.

Quiet fell. No engine noise, no tire noise. Quiet for the first time. Jesse gaped through all the windows. Nothing around—no building, no cars, no people—just us, in this car, incongruous on the desert floor. We watched as cops massed on the road below.

I unlatched my door and pushed it open. I sat stock still. I had stopped thinking. My heart still pounded. I wanted to scream. The red blood splattered on the passing windshield flickered in my head. In the rearview mirror, men pointed rifles at us. Later, people asked me what was going through my head. Nothing. I just *did.* Not even instinctual—but robotic, self-activating. I lifted my hand. It did not shake, but I felt so weak that holding it up took effort. I let it drop. The fresh air through the open door cooled me. I looked over at Louisa. Cindy had buried her head in Louisa's shoulder. The little girl's chest heaved up and down. Louisa's head lay against Cindy's, eyes closed, slowly rocking, still smeared with tears.

I didn't look back at Jesse. I knew the gun still pointed at my back. I felt Paul's fear; I didn't have to see it.

I set my foot on the ground outside. The subtle shift felt like a small earthquake inside the car. Everyone jerked in surprise and waited. I did not move. I sat awkwardly still with one foot outside the car. From the road, it must have looked very strange. They probably jumped to attention, guns snapped to. I was more worried about Jesse. I waited. He didn't move. He didn't say anything. I inhaled, realizing I'd been holding my breath. I looked behind me. An army of cops lined the roadway. I set the other foot outside and stood, my back to the road. From the corner of my eye I saw Jesse lean forward to see me.

"What are you doing?"

"I have to talk to 'em," I said.

"They got guns."

So do you, I thought as I turned to face the road. I raised my hands and eyed the wall of policemen. I could still see Jesse slumped low in his seat, staring desperately out the back window. Paul had closed his eyes.

I stood there, arms outstretched, waiting. I didn't think they'd shoot me. I don't know why. Jesse had taken a few bucks and assumed he'd be shot. I had done… what I had done… and assumed I would not. Privilege and innocence walked hand-in-hand.

There was movement on the road below. A few figures scurried back and forth along the police line, keeping low. After a minute or so, a dark-suited man rounded one of the cars. He stood upright, his arms extended like mine to show that he didn't have a gun. He stopped for a moment as if to make sure I took it all in, and then began walking up the rise toward the car. Raising my arms higher, I bent down to see Jesse.

"Let me talk to 'em," I said, looking him in the eye and hoping that would calm him.

"I ain't goin' back," he said.

I couldn't address the caged animal panic in his eye. "Just let me talk to 'em."

He pulled the gun close to his chest and wrapped both hands around it.

"You comin' back?" he asked.

"Yeah. I'll be back."

I turned toward the road and walked, arms outstretched, very slowly. I stared at the cop as we approached each other. He was tall. Looked to be around fifty and his face was sad, not his expression, but his features. They telegraphed weariness. As I approached, he carefully opened his suit jacket in another show of disarmament. It was strange, this slow dance toward each other—like a reverse old west gunfight. This time the shooting came first.

A few yards away from him, I let my hands fall and he did the same. I stopped close enough to talk, but far enough that he couldn't grab me. We eyed each other. He bit his lower lip in something that, under the circumstances, suggested a smile.

"Down there," he said, nodding back to the knot of cops, "they told me they had sharpshooters ready. I told them we didn't know who to shoot." This was his ice-breaker.

"There's always me," I said, my attempt at a show of ease as feeble as his.

"What's your name?"

"Lennie."

"I'm Loewy. I'm a cop. What's your last name?"

"Ashland."

"Who shot the gun, Lennie?" He got right to it.

My tears surprised me. I felt them before I knew I was crying. Blood inside the car like sloshed paint on the cracked and shattered glass. I gasped for breath, trying to hold it in.

"It wasn't loaded," I pleaded.

"What do you mean?"

"He didn't have any bullets."

"Who? Slow down," Loewy said. He extended his arm as if to place it on my shoulder, but we were too far away and he let it drop. I took a few deep breaths. "That's it," he said, calming me. "Who shot the gun?"

"Jesse."

"The one who held up the gas station?"

"Yes."

"Who else is in the car?"

"Me, Louisa and Paul and Cindy."

"Cindy, the little girl from the restaurant."

"Yes."

"What are Paul and Louisa's last names?"

"Benton and Haas. Louisa Haas."

"Is anyone in the car hurt?"

I shook my head.

"Now tell me what happened."

I told him about meeting Jesse at the gas station, about the ride and the restaurant. Recounting it, I tried to make it seem sensible, sort of inevitable, like it was at the time—just the... banality of it. But hearing myself, I knew that I failed. I barely believed me.

"You gave him back the gun?" he asked when I'd finished.

"After I saw he didn't have any bullets," I protested. "It was just a hunk of metal. It didn't matter."

"Why did you believe him?"

"I don't know... There wasn't any reason not to. He was just a kid." My arms flailed as I tried to explain. "He was just a kid," I repeated in weak self-defense. "He wasn't gonna hurt anyone."

I swiped at the tears with my sleeve and then shuddered as if I'd only just heard my last statement. "The blood in the police car..."

Loewy paused a moment, nodding. He stared at the ground, kicked a small rock. His hands sank into his pants pockets. "Don't worry about that right now," he said.

"Someone got shot. What happened?"

The pause continued. "It should be okay."

I sighed with relief. It might not be as bad as I thought.

"What's Jesse's last name?" asked Loewy.

"I don't know," I admitted, again feeling foolish at not knowing something so fundamental and realizing how careless I had been.

"Did he say where he came from?"

"He sounded local at the gas station, like he came from around there?"

"How old would you say?"

"About sixteen, I think."

"And he still has the gun?"

I nodded.

"What does he want?"

I shook my head, impotent. "I don't know... to get away. He was running. Just going."

"Where? To what? You must have some idea."

"He asked where we were going. We told him California, and he liked that. He asked if he could come." I almost laughed it sounded so outlandish. "He sincerely asked, like we could say 'no,' like he didn't have a gun pointed at us."

"I thought you said he didn't have bullets?"

"Not at the beginning. At the beginning we thought he did. Only later, he told me he didn't and showed me the empty gun, like he'd been faking it the whole time."

"You told him he could go with you?

I nodded. "I think he has to get somewhere. The ocean, I said. He wanted to go. Maybe it'll be okay if we can take him there. It's where the three of us were going."

"Can I talk to him?"

I looked up at the stillness surrounding the car and imagined Jesse huddled in the back seat cradling the gun to his chest.

"I don't think he'll let you. He was terrified of the cops. Kept saying they'd kill him."

"Will he let anybody go? The little girl. Could you convince him?"

"We tried that. He said you'd kill us if we let her go."

"But he talks to you."

"Yeah."

"He trusts you."

"I think so."

He stopped asking questions and looked up at the car sitting god-forsaken and foolish on the desert dirt and rock.

"What happens now?" I asked.

Loewy eyed the cops on the road. "I'm not sure," he mumbled.

He was thinking. I waited, anxious, desperate for someone's practical wisdom to drag me out of this hole I'd dug.

"It's gonna be up to you," he said. "You'll have to talk him down. Can you?"

"I don't know."

"That's not what I need to hear."

I tried to consider, really assess it, but I couldn't think. There was no rational answer. All I could do was lie to him.

"Yes," I said.

"Wait here." He turned and rushed back toward the road. I resisted the urge to chase after him, begging him not to leave me alone. Instead, I stood as still as my fear would let me. I waited. When he reached the police line, other cops ran to him. He pointed and spoke as men fell away, executing orders. After a couple of minutes, he jogged back toward me, carrying a small box.

He handed me a radio and told me what to do. And then he said it.

"I don't know if I'm doing the right thing, but something in me says you oughta know. I didn't tell you the truth a while ago. A policeman died in the car. Jesse killed him."

The world shifted. I felt dizzy and thought I might throw up. I leaned forward with my hands on my knees. I wanted to run—as far and as fast as I could. I could have kept going and going.

"You okay?" Loewy asked.

I willed myself upright.

"You've got to do this," Loewy said, nodding his head for emphasis.

"I know," I replied.

"A cop is dead," he repeated gravely, "and the only thing keeping the rest of 'em from taking you all out is that little girl. She's buying you time for now."

He stared at me, making sure it sunk in. It had.

I walked up the rise, radio in hand. The car looked like an odd metal prison as I approached the open driver side door. It took enormous effort, like lifting dead weight, to bend forward and look inside. My body rebelled. When I did, I had never seen fear like that. Louisa and Cindy wept. Paul had his face in his hands as if trying to blot it all out. Jesse was cradling his gun like a teddy bear, his finger on the trigger.

I had to force myself to confront the terror inside the car, force my mouth to form words. Everything in me said to run.

"What's that?" Jesse asked of the box. He used the gun to point at it.

"It's a radio." Trying to soothe, I sounded like a children's TV show host, but I didn't care. I had enough to do to coerce myself back behind the wheel. "A radio so we can talk to 'em."

"Paul." He didn't respond. "Paul," I repeated. Again, nothing. Once he pulled his hands from his face and showed his eyes I wished he hadn't. They were drained. Looking in them, I knew the person behind them would be no use. I had hoped that he would help me through this, but he was gone. When I turned to Louisa, her eyes met mine, questioning, imploring, as if to pull some of the burden and take it as her own. I felt relieved to know that I was not all alone.

"Paul, why don't you move on up front?" I said.

He looked at Jesse.

"It's okay, Jesse. We'll all sit up here and you'll have the whole back seat." I nodded at Jesse to coax an affirmative response. His head flicked imperceptibly. Paul glanced at me and I motioned him to move. He moved to open the door, and I shook my head angrily and motioned him to climb over the seat. Louisa scooted to the center of the front bench as he did.

I took the driver's seat. I settled the radio on top of the dashboard and started the car.

"Where we goin'?" Jesse asked, surprisingly calm.

"California," I replied. I watched him in the rearview mirror as I put the car in gear and crept forward across the desert ground. He accepted it. Head low, he peered out the windows, wary, but he accepted it. I don't know what he thought was happening. Maybe he thought we were going to California.

IX

Ten years later when I went to see him, during my second grand quest for meaning, Loewy had retired and lived alone outside Flagstaff. His wife had died a few years before, but his children lived nearby and that seemed to keep him in good spirits. He must have been in his sixties—in good health. He surprised me when I called; he seemed pleased to hear from me. I had a hard time getting off the phone, as if he would have happily relived the whole episode, long-distance, right then and there.

Ushering me into his small house with a vigorous handshake and a big smile he said, "You don't look too worse for wear."

He offered me a drink, which I accepted. Once he'd poured and settled himself in a chair, he looked puzzled for a moment. "I think I've been waiting for you," he said, as though the idea surprised even him. "I never got the sense that it was finished."

I raised a silent "Amen" to that one.

"It was the only time in my police career," he continued, "when I was sure of absolutely nothing. That's why I remember it so much. That cop, that was a tragedy. The kind of thing you just go over and over knowing, knowing that somehow it didn't have to happen." He shook his head at the memory.

I was glad to hear that what happened seemed as significant, as grandiose, to someone else as it did to me. It made me feel less like the childish dreamer. I reminded him that I'd come to learn about events I wasn't party to. I needed to know what had led up to that bloody end.

I also needed, I admitted, independent verification that I had not, like Mrs. Gerald, revised my history to blunt my own guilt.

"I need to know," I told him, "if what I think happened is what really did. And I need to know why… how much was me and how much just… happened."

He laughed at me. "You were a Harvard boy, right? Yeah. I can hear it. One of my nephews went to one o' those schools, not Harvard but some muckymuck… 'What I *think* happened.' It happened to *you*. What does thinking have to do with it?"

He considered it hilarious that I questioned the very reality of my own experience. And he was right. It's what had gotten me into trouble in the first place. But with a 'what the hell' gesture, he dove in.

"I was the first detective there, at the restaurant. At first, it was just a missing girl and the uniform guys were handling it, but when we heard about you folks, and tied it in with the gas station, I got involved. I was local so I got it before the Feds.

"I didn't know what to make of it. What didn't make sense was this guy kidnapping you all, and then you wind up in a restaurant with him, sitting in a booth, chatting up a little girl. That immediately made me think, and pardon me for saying so, that you had something more to do with him. The station guy said that one of you was wearing a Harvard T-shirt, which made it stranger still. You didn't see a lot of those around there. So I've got a kid holding up gas stations and three others who might be helping? I don't know. Then there's the fact that the guy… what was his name?"

"Jesse."

"Yeah. He gets pennies from the robbery and sounds like a total fuckup, pardon my French, when it comes to thieving." He took a moment to wonder at it. "It was strange. Half monkey show, half dead serious. That explosion left a huge crater where the gas pumps had been. Destroyed the place, like someone dropped a bomb. And then there was a little girl missing. We had no idea who the gunman was, or who you were. So we assumed the worst, like we had to do. We assumed you took the girl."

It was still hard hearing myself discussed as someone who'd abduct a child.

"We put the girl's picture out everywhere, and got a bunch of calls from folks at another restaurant. Again with the restaurants. You're robbing gas stations—that's what we're thinking—and stealing little girls and then going out for bites to eat. Made no sense. I think that's where I got sloppy. It's not what I expected from dangerous bank robbers and kidnappers. It was more *Katzenjammer Kids.* Talking to the girl's parents, we knew there was trouble on the home front. Other folks said they saw the girl walk out alone, and that was *after* you folks had already left. I thought that if she left after you, maybe she just walked away and you had nothing to do with it. It all seemed so damned sloppy." He smiled in wonderment at the nonsensicality. "I guess I stopped taking it that seriously."

Then he looked right at me—one in a series of looks or words that I read as accusatory. "I had not expected that shot," he said before averting his eyes. His face changed. The jovial air disappeared and every one of his sixty-plus years clouded his eyes.

"It blew everything apart. I heard the noise, knew what it was, knew it was a shot, but I didn't know the circumstances. Then the radio chatter started, all the yelling and questions. I grabbed my receiver, trying to get someone to tell me what the hell was goin' on. But that just added to the confusion. Suddenly, it was like someone turned the volume down. The hysteria died and the radio cleared. Someone said a man was hit. A head shot, from your car. What was downright silly turned a 180. It was for real now. Life and death."

* * *

With Loewy's radio sitting on the dashboard, I drove across the jagged landscape, headed for the road. I pulled the radio handset and pushed the button. "We're ready," I spoke into it.

"Go ahead," a muddy voice replied.

We jostled across the desert floor until we hit the road. As we did, the roadblock cleared away and two police cars pulled out in front of us as several more got in line behind.

"They're comin', too," I explained, noting the surprised faces. "I guess everyone wants to go." I tried to smile, as if the joke could be appreciated.

"What's happening?" Paul asked.

"We're gonna drive through. They've got a special route for us. All we have to do is tell 'em if we need anything, and they'll get it for us."

"What are they gonna do when we get there?" Paul demanded.

"The important thing," I replied, "is to get there, right?" I stomped on the last word and tried to catch his eye, but failed. I could have hit him. He was making things worse.

The radio crackled. "Cindy. Cindy?"

I handed Louisa the receiver.

"This is your momma, honey," came from the radio.

"Just push the button to talk," I said.

Louisa did so and held it up to Cindy, who remained silent. "Go ahead," Louisa prodded.

"Hello?" Cindy spoke as if the receiver might bite.

"This is your momma."

Cindy did not respond. She looked through the windshield at the train of police cars.

"Are you all right?"

"Yeah," replied Cindy. "I'm fine."

"Everything's gonna be alright, honey. No one's gonna hurt you."

"I know. Is Daddy there?"

"I'm here," said a man's voice. "I love you, baby."

"I love you, too," Cindy replied.

There was nothing more. Louisa handed me the receiver.

The police led us to a minor road. It looked barely wide enough for two cars, but I could see the faint white line down the middle. The road was empty. Just us, with police cars in front and behind. In the near distance, the faint, dull chop of helicopter blades.

None of us spoke. I had never dreamt this level of surreal. Three abreast in the car's front seat—Cindy on Louisa's lap—all close enough to feel each other's fearful shuddering. In the back, Jesse cradled his gun.

I had no idea where this road led. I just knew I had no choice but to follow it. All I could do, driving down this narrow lane with a gun at my back and three blameless lives next to mine, was hope that Loewy could get us out unharmed. I refused to consider that he really expected me to end this. Those were just words, I told myself, designed to buck me up. He couldn't expect someone like me, a child just yesterday, to juggle all of this, life and death, but for real this time, not some manufactured college boy fever dream. Blood had splattered on windshields this time.

Time stopped. Everything was new. The pavement we drove on and the sloping desert surrounding us didn't look normal anymore. Nothing was normal. Breathing wasn't even normal. It felt deliberate, like I might stop if I didn't concentrate on doing it. Everything had been transformed. I stared past the police cars at the empty, narrow road ahead. We entered an endlessness. There was no destination. I dreaded stopping and I dreaded going on. During the purgatorial span of the Midwest landscape, anxious with anticipation, I'd waited for something to happen. Now, I dreaded it. Each glance loaded, I avoided everyone's eyes. Louisa trained hers on me for seconds at a time, seeking reassurance or a simple human connection, but I kept mine dead ahead and tried to will her to stop. Her stares felt like sunlight through a magnifying glass trained on my skin. Eventually she turned away, and I sighed with relief inside. I did not want to have to soothe or coddle. I wanted to disappear somewhere. If I had to do it right there inside the car, so be it. I went where I had to go to get through this and I resented anyone trying to drag me back. I stared past the police cars at the empty road ahead.

Unnervingly, dragging me out of my abstraction, the chopper noise intensified. In the windows and mirrors, I couldn't see anything until a brightly painted bird covered with huge letters whizzed past the car so low we instinctually ducked. The police helicopter zoomed after it. I pounded on the wheel in frustration and grabbed the radio receiver.

"What's all the noise?" I hissed furiously. All of my pent-up anger exploded at what I considered a breach of promise. I should have been terrified, but dragged from my cocoon, I was mad.

"It's a news helicopter," Loewy assured. "Don't worry. We're getting rid of it."

Before the receiver went dead, he yelled, "Get that goddamned..."

Again, I sat on alert, nerves tingling, heart racing. I could have wept. I desperately wanted a respite from this and longed to return to the void of the narrow, empty road that I could passively follow—like another dance with Fate, only this time asking nothing of Her, and hoping She'd take pity enough to offer it.

The news chopper made another pass. A cameraman hung out the doorway, pointing his lens into the car. The chopper turned around to film the passenger side. It seemed to zero in on Jesse. He looked at it and rolled down the window. Thrilled at a clean shot, the helicopter moved even closer. Jesse pointed his gun at the cameraman, who instantly dropped his rig, both arms waving manically as he screamed "UP! UP! Move!" The helicopter veered spectacularly and sped away. I heard a *pop* as it did so. Jesse pulled off a parting shot—his goodbye.

Cindy giggled. Louisa smothered a smile.

"Hey," Jesse said, holding up the gun and watching the helicopter disappear. "I could get pretty good at this."

* * *

"I had no idea," Loewy said. "I don't think we knew how we'd handle it. I was stalling for time. Mainly 'cause I believed you, even though I wasn't sure if I should. After I talked to you, they hit me with every question that I didn't have time to get the answer to. I gave 'em your names and what I could about the one with the gun. I told 'em to check you out. We were on tribal land. Did you know that? We were. It complicated things. Someone else had to smooth that over. We needed the tribal folks to help get you a route—didn't matter where, just somewhere. I trusted you after we talked, but I knew, by the book, that I shouldn't have.

"Once I got you back on the road, I hoped it would keep your gunman... Jesse... that was his name, right? Hoping it would keep him calm while we figured how to disarm him or take him down. The main thing was keeping the little girl safe. Frankly, you folks came second. We still couldn't be sure you were totally clean, so we focused on the little girl—the one sure thing we had. We couldn't go wrong if we focused on protecting her.

"When I talked to you that first time, the girl's mother and father were waiting in the car. I had to bring 'em along. At the station—when she heard that we found you—the mother made a big scene. Threatened to go out and scream to the press if we didn't take her. Plus, I figured the parents might calm the girl and lock down an ID, so I brought 'em.

"When I got back in the car, of course the parents are there. She jumps all over me. 'Where's Cindy? Where's my little girl?' I try to explain that we're taking it one step at a time, that we're trying to keep her safe, but she won't shut up. Then she sees you guys moving and has a fit. 'Where they going? They're leaving! Stop them.' So I'm watching you and trying to make sure all the black and whites are where they're supposed to be, and all the while tellin' this woman what we're doing so she'll shut up and let me think, and at the same time her husband keeps saying to her, 'Can you just calm down, please!'

"Then, outta nowhere, that fuckin' news helicopter showed up. Dove down at the car like a hawk at a bunny. I didn't even hear the shot. One of my guys told me that the camera flew out the door. I want to laugh now, but then, I didn't have a clue what to make of it. Now this guy's takin' potshots out the window? That didn't sound good, even if it was at a news helicopter. Hell, I could've shot at it myself.

"Can I get you another drink?" he asked, rising to freshen his. He poured us both and resumed his seat. "Looking at you now," he said, squinting as if searching my face for hidden clues, "it's hard to think of you as that same person." He smiled and pointed between us like he was drawing a line. "It's hard to think that it really happened and that you and me were in the middle of it. It was the biggest thing I'd ever seen as a cop. I'd done stakeouts, drug busts, investigated... everything. But nothing like this. At more than one point I was sure it would end my career. I actually thought about that. We were off the reservation—as the expression goes. No rule book for this. Groping in the dark. Now I'm sittin' across from you with a couple of scotches in our hands. It just gets wilder."

He leaned back and made himself comfortable. "It didn't take long to get information on all of you, and it was clean. Harvard graduates, solid citizens—at least to my mind. I had a captain who saw the same stuff I did, but wouldn't let go of the idea that you were some kind of spoiled rich kids gone bad. He was sure of it. Smelled it. We found your gunman in a town near the gas station. Had a juvenile record. Some vandalism, petty theft. Nothing with guns or violence, so my captain figured you folks tipped him over the edge. It's amazing how one notion just led naturally to another, no matter that the first one was wrong. You build on it and build on it until it's too big to tear down.

"'It's not him you need to worry about,' the captain told me. 'It's the ones in the car with him. He's nothing. He'd never do something this big. They're the ones.'

"His mother wouldn't come. The Oklahoma cops talked to her, and they wanted to bring her out. They thought it would help to reach him, but she wouldn't. Said she acted like it wasn't her concern. He had left home and that was that. Didn't sound like she had much to do with him when he was around. The father was long gone.

"The captain refused to believe that little girl just happened to go to your car. One notion on top of another. He thought this was all a big joke with you folks—that we were a big joke and that you were using that Jesse as a dupe." Loewy sighed. "He was a good man, good cop. And he was right as often as not. When I got off that radio with him, I went back over everything we said… your face, gestures, trying to decide if he was right, if I was right. I couldn't. I just didn't know. You seemed for real when we talked. Sincere. I thought you were really broken up, but, believe it or not, the Harvard thing kept creepin' up, that you folks were smart enough to fake anything. It was like you were magic, or… or witches or somethin' and got thrills from messin' with cops, misleading us, making chaos and getting away with whatever you could.

"I didn't know. I'm sorry to say now. It's kinda embarrassing, but he put doubts in my head. I would have done things differently if he hadn't. Some of the worst might not have happened."

He sipped his drink. "Do you still see any o' those folks, your friends in the car?"

I shook my head. "No," I replied. "We lost touch."

"I had high hopes," he said reflectively. "When you stopped that last time, I thought you'd finally reached him. I thought to myself it would be over soon, and that it would be all right. Then I saw your face. You looked done in. More than that. I don't know how to describe it. You looked like it was over. For you. That you couldn't do it anymore. When I saw your face, I just… died a little."

X

To call something fantastic or unbelievable is different from saying it's like a dream. Saying something's like a dream suggests an experience of fluidity and grace, a processional stateliness never achieved during our chaotic waking hours. But, in truth, dreams might be jagged, staccato or wild, like exploding roman candles with French New Wave cinema jump cuts left and right.

This was the most poetic notion of dreams. Tan desert all around us, a caravan of cars roaming at 30 miles per hour, as if dazed, like a funeral procession that had lost its way.

I'd call on the radio if we needed anything—food or a bathroom. If Cindy and Louisa needed the latter, they'd stop the caravan for a few minutes and we'd sit in the road and wait while they decided where to take them to find a bathroom that could be sufficiently cleared of all signs of life. Then we'd get a call on the radio and the whole procession would limp forward again as they led us to a deserted gas station or little store that sat as forlorn and ghostlike as everything else around us. There, they'd let Cindy and Louisa use the toilet. They did the same for us unless we only had to pee. In that case, the caravan would stop, and either Paul or I would march a few yards into the desert with rifle barrels trained on us all around. Jesse did everything directly on the opposite side of the car from the police line. He defecated two feet from the car door.

They brought us food. We'd ask for something, and after a while, the procession would stop. The police cars ahead always left an empty zone between us and them. Cops jogged into the zone and placed the food on the road. Once they were safely back behind the barricades, I went out to get the food and brought it back to the car. It was particularly surreal at night. They used car headlights to illuminate the no man's land of the middle of the road in the blackened desert—an oasis of light in the pitch black night that disappeared the moment I shut my car door.

As we started driving again after the second such stop, Jesse said, "I guess no one's laughin' at me now, huh?" They were among the few words he'd spoken in almost a day. For the next twelve hours, he barely said another word. Nobody did. I knew I was supposed to be talking to him, trying to calm him down, but I couldn't. I couldn't even try. I thought about doing it, the necessity, the duty—I thought about it all the time, but I couldn't. I avoided his gaze when it landed on me, and it often did, as if he was waiting, as if he thought I had some answers that I selfishly kept to myself.

I didn't.

We crawled across the desert in silence. We stopped to pee and get food. Louisa and I took turns driving. We might have been going in circles. It was like a dream. Near the middle of the second day, Jesse spoke again:

"How much further?" he asked.

"Not that far, really," I lied, having no idea.

I talked to Loewy again. I left the car and we met in the road, what seemed like a thousand headlights blaring at us. He asked if everyone was okay, what progress I'd made. Again I lied. I told him that I had tried to engage Jesse, tried to talk to him, but that he remained largely mute and sullen. He did, but so did I. He sulked in the back seat, and I in the front.

My mind wandered. I thought back to New York, my old world, so different from this. Speeding metal, concrete, and giant buildings had been to me what rocks and scrub brush had become. So utterly different. I had considered those man-made things natural; they had sprouted from the earth as organically as rock. It comforted me to think back on it because it was artificial and unnatural, predictable; it was home; scar-toughened skin, weathered and beaten, so often wounded and healed over that it felt impervious. Nothing could touch or harm it. This, out here, this was like raw nerves, infant skin exposed to every gust, pest, and change in the weather, tender as a rose. That was part of its beauty—its fragility. And here I had become equally exposed, so much so that I had withdrawn to the past, hypnotized by the faint white line and the car engine's gentle roar, floating, like a lazy boy on a raft, eyes closed, an aimless hitcher on the back of the world.

On the night of the second day, as the car rolled down another identical road, as the dream stretched along the endless asphalt we traveled like catatonics chasing a ball of yarn, Jesse spoke.

"I don't wanna drive no more," he said.

I woke up. The dream, its comfortable nothingness, its aimless digression—it ended. The situation grew palpable again. We had stopped at a gas station and met a boy… there was an explosion… and a little girl… blood had splattered. There it was again, like the room's stale air on waking. With my hands on the wheel, I turned to Jesse, ignoring the road ahead of me.

"Why not, Jesse?"

He shrugged. "Just don't wanna."

His face showed resignation, if not hopelessness. He still clutched the gun in his lap.

Louisa looked at me, questioning. I had not seen Paul's eyes in two days. He had disappeared more completely than I.

"Stop the car," Jesse said.

"Let me call 'em and tell 'em what we're doing, okay?"

"No. Stop. Stop now."

I hit the brakes. Immediately Loewy's voice on the radio. I lunged for the receiver and pushed the transmit button.

"No. Not here," Jesse insisted. "Up there. Go!"

He indicated the desert off to the side of the road. I turned and drove. As soon as I dared hope, I asked, "Is this okay?"

"No. More." I kept my finger on the button, hoping Loewy would hear it all.

"I need to tell 'em what's going on, Jesse."

He didn't respond. I raised the receiver. "We're going to stop now," I said into it. "Just like before."

"Okay," Loewy said. "Take it slow."

About fifty yards from the road, I stopped. I turned off the headlights and the engine. Deep silence without the engine; empty darkness without the headlights. Stillness and silence for a good thirty seconds as we waited, getting used to the lack of light and sound.

"Let's talk in person," Loewy squawked through the receiver.

"No. Stay here," Jesse ordered.

"Jesse wants to talk to me. I'll get back."

I hung up. I waited, staring forward to avoid even the semblance of pressuring him. The silence ominous, like before a verdict. Was he done? Was he ready to give up? Was he done with us? At that moment, I didn't think he'd kill. Terror had prompted that cop's shooting, and he seemed calm now, as far as I could tell.

I hadn't been paying attention. I had ignored Paul all day. I had recognized how effectively he had disappeared, huddled in his corner by the door, and I had let him be. I saw him rise up. I was surprised by the overhead light popping on before I realized the door had flown open. Louisa uttered something as she shifted confusedly to get out of the way. And then he flew out of the car. I heard tumbling and then footfalls, running. For a moment I caught sight of his back. The front seat crashed forward, throwing Louisa and Cindy as Jesse charged out the open door after him, gun aloft. He shot twice into the dark. He fell to his knees to keep himself out of the cops' sight, but it was too dark. He couldn't see anything. Paul was gone.

I grabbed the radio. "It's okay. It's okay!" I shouted into it. "Nobody's hurt. Paul ran." I realize now that I didn't know if anyone was hurt. Jesse could have shot Paul for all I knew, but there was no noise, no screams. In movies people screamed or moaned when they got shot. It's all I had to go on.

Cindy jumped into Louisa's lap. They both looked more surprised than scared. Jesse slowly lowered his gun, but it was still half aloft and pointing our way when he returned to the back seat. Again we settled in a state of disbelief.

"Son of a bitch left us here," Jesse complained. He sounded hurt. Ironic that he was the one to say it, because I felt the same, and judging from Louisa's stunned expression, so did she. "I can't believe he left us here."

He said 'us.' He still considered himself part of 'us.' That was good. I didn't even know why, but it gave me hope.

"Where did he go?" Cindy asked.

I looked down at the line of cops.

"Pick it up," Louisa said. The radio had been cackling. I grabbed it.

"It's okay," I said again.

"What happened?" It was Loewy.

"Paul," I said. "He ran."

"Where?"

"Don't know. Dove out of the car and ran."

"The shots?"

"Just… just nothing. Didn't hit anything. He's out there."

"We need to talk," he said.

"Just a little time. Just a little. I'll call you in a minute."

I needed the time. I was confused. Louisa subtly shook her head as if to clear it. He had abandoned us. Even if 'us' was only me, him, and Louisa, he had abandoned us. Despite all of my brooding and isolation, this remained, to me, a communal affair. *We* had done this. *We* were experiencing this bit of madness. Part of my belief in our ability to survive was the 'we.'

Paul had crushed that. After thinking about it a moment, it seemed comical. He had quite literally *bailed.*

"I guess this means divorce," I said.

"Tell me about it," Louisa seconded. "I can't believe he did that. I mean, really. I can't believe it." For a moment, the fact of Jesse and his gun disappeared. It was just me sitting with a college friend having an, 'Oh my God!' moment. For the first time in days, I looked Louisa in the eye. I smiled for the first time in just as long.

"What do you say to this?" she asked rhetorically. "It's really so him that you'd never expect him to be honest enough to do it."

"It's like the version of him he spent his life trying to pretend he wasn't. He even had us convinced."

I did feel hurt. I'd known him since freshman year, back when he wore bad shoes and an awkward self-consciousness about his middle-class, public school, never-been-outside-the-country upbringing. He was a nerdy guy seeking cool by proxy and decided that I was it. We'd been best friends ever since. There had always been artifice about him, but this was Harvard—we were all lousy with it. In Paul, though, you got the sense that there wasn't an authentic self to settle into. Or, more accurately, not one that he could live with or bear to show the world.

I had thought our bond was stronger than this; because of that, I felt the fool. For the second time in a week, I felt the fool.

"What'd he do that for?" Jesse groused, genuinely pained.

I turned to him, and as I saw the gun propped on his lap, I slammed back into this world. The bath of easy intimacy drained. Louisa again became a disorienting stranger to whom I didn't know what to say. The world of Jesse and his gun precluded all others.

"He got scared," I soothed. "He just got scared."

"You don't run off when you're scared."

"I know. I've got to go talk to them now, Jesse."

After a moment, he nodded assent.

I turned the car headlights on and opened my door. I stepped out slowly with my hands far from my sides and walked toward the road.

XI

Louisa and I had spoken a couple of times and she had written me several letters in the year or so following. But I stopped replying. I imagined she wanted explanations and I didn't have any. I imagined she was waiting to air recriminations that I couldn't withstand. I imagined she would remind me of failures with which I hadn't yet come to terms.

Of course, that didn't stop me from resenting the fact that she hadn't come to the hospital in person, despite my unresponsiveness. I feared seeing her, but I wanted her to want to see me. Her desire to do so would have allayed my fear. In other words, the usual jumble of wants and not-wants, 'come heres' and 'go aways.'

She didn't come; I didn't respond. Time passed. Ten years. Since I saved the hardest for last, she was either second or third to the last on my list of people to interview. With her, it wasn't a simple interrogation. Half of me considered it the prodigal's return.

She lived in Los Angeles. I wrote and asked how she had been and if I could come. Guess what? She didn't respond. I suppose it was her turn this time. I went anyway.

I had her home address but thought it less invasive to ambush her at work. She was headmistress at a tony West Side LA girls' school. That was no surprise. It seemed just right—bordering on 'the expected,' but without that term's negative connotations. She had been true to herself. She had proven that the young woman I had known was far less of a pose than the young man I had been. There was, even at that time, an essential Louisa that had not radically altered. I took comfort in that. I was happy for her.

Standing outside the school, I watched the pretty young things pour out at the end of a day. I had been to LA before, and its shimmer always dumbfounded me. The place glistened. The light beckoned. It promised. Leaves are that much greener, shadows deeper, reflections that much brighter, even one's own. Possibility blanches the place. I imagine it's easy to live there in hope… hope of change, success, riches, love. The light in your eyes lets you imagine the world as you want it to be, as opposed to settling for it as it is. The place is sadly fantastical.

The tanned blonde girls flitted through the door, still sharp in their crisp blue uniforms, barely rumpled or askew from the day's rigors, proof of how much attention had been paid to grooming during its course. Dots of color interrupted the blonde, white-skinned avalanche. Just enough color such that the eye usually glimpsed one or two—the proper number.

I sipped a large coffee and leaned comfortably, knowing it might take an hour for the headmistress to finish her day and find her way out. Watching the comings and goings around the school, I realized I hadn't seen this much natural fiber since college. Even in downtown Santa Fe, there's the tourist and regular folk contingent. Workers there aren't the elite, and they don't try to fake it. It's not the land of dreams, so they can't imagine themselves internet millionaires or reality TV stars. Here, everyone stands poised to snatch the dream, should it saunter by.

Finally, I saw her. She looked exactly the same. I laughed to myself. I had been wondering if LA conferred immortality to those who prostrated themselves at her feet. Now it looked as though that might be the case. She stopped when she recognized me. Astonished, her mouth opened. And after a moment, the "O" turned into a smile, briefly, even fleetingly, but it did. She recognized something old and familiar and instinctively smiled. And then she remembered the blood and the fear, and the smile went away. She looked quickly from side to side as if searching for someplace to hide. I stepped forward to block her escape.

"Hi," I said. Her lips were still parted in surprise; her expression didn't change. It was as if I hadn't spoken. And then, like plaster cracking, her mouth moved, the corners turned up a bit. "I'm sorry to attack, but frankly, I was afraid if I kept asking, you'd say no. So I didn't ask."

She looked me up and down. I started feeling hopeful, and then she smiled outright. She opened her arms and I fell into them. She even smelled the same. Pulling away, she wiped tears from her eyes.

"For a moment," she confessed, "I was afraid of… not this." She indicated her own teary eyes. I understood. I think we both feared that there would be nothing left, no sense that we once loved each other. We feared that what we'd seen and learned of me—the fear, and the foolishness and the havoc it could wreak—that it would have destroyed the bond we had. But that wasn't the case. I still saw my friend and she still saw me. My own eyes filled.

I followed her to a little shop, where she ordered a pastry for us to share—the kind of thing she used to do.

She got right to it. "Why didn't you write back?" she asked.

"Why didn't you come see me anyway?" I implored right back at her.

That dispensed with the recriminations portion of the reunion. Equally guilty, we both had explaining to do.

"Shame," I confessed. "What I'm scared I put us through. God. Think about it. Even now, it's… beyond belief." Sitting across from her in an LA coffee shop, ten years later, I saw the bullet shatter a man's head and splatter his blood all over. My heart pounded again from the fear. My hand trembled, and I sloppily set my cup down.

"This is why," I said to her as I tried to control myself. "It's why I ran." I looked at her. "It's real again. Looking at you."

Talking to Loewy and Mrs. Gerald, that had been research. This was much more.

"Had you omitted it, blocked it out?"

I shook my head. "Just shaded it. There, but vague, like a story I heard again and again, but a little less than real."

She touched my hand.

"When you didn't write back or call, after your mother told me you'd be okay, I let it go. Let you go. I never shoved it back or anything. It's always been there, but I guess I was relieved not seeing you. I could walk away from it, like an old dress I left behind. I have to admit, I think you did me a favor by not answering. It's what let me walk away."

"Good. After all that happened, I owed you a favor."

We smiled at that.

"Where'd you go?" she asked.

"Bummed around for a while. Took a couple of jobs trying to be someone else, landed in New Mexico. Been there ever since."

"Why there?"

I thought a moment. "It all happened out west, near there. That landscape, the sky. It burned me up, like lighting. That place did so much to me, exposed so much in me that I couldn't turn away. It owned me." I smiled. "That makes no sense."

"Yes it does. What do you do?"

"I have horses!" I announced buoyantly, knowing it would be the last thing she'd expect and a happy change of subject.

"What?"

"Real, live, great big horses. Four of 'em. Others come and go. I rescue 'em and adopt 'em out."

She shook her head in mild disbelief. "That's new. You never even had a cat."

"Yeah. I've moved on from people," I said.

"Married?" she asked.

"No. Much the loner. There are people in the horse community I see. Ride with them and work with them on rescues and the like, but no. Very little long term. Damaged goods here, darlin'. What about you?"

"Yes. Married. Eight years in."

I nodded appreciatively. "You love him?"

"Yes, but not in the way you mean."

"How do you know what way I mean? Even I don't."

"Not in the lucky way."

"What's that?"

"The 'soul mate' thing. The ridiculous bond between you. The 'I'd be lost without you' way. This is the 'good, kind man' way. The usual way."

"What makes you say that?"

"I know you. Still. You'd want it to be a grand passion."

I scowled, unconvinced, even as I proved her point. "Why didn't you hold out?" I asked.

"Same reason you turned to livestock. We went through almost the same thing, you and I. You retreated from the world. I found safe harbor."

"Success?"

"Yes."

"Good. Kids?"

"One. He's five."

"Happy?"

"Enough."

We covered ten years' essentials in a very short time.

"What's all this about, Lennie? The reunion…"

"You know I talked to Loewy and Cindy's mother. That was trying to understand what I couldn't see. This is trying to… I guess resurrect the rest of me. The old me. I cut everything off. Like I never went to college and never knew you or Paul. Like I never took an ill-advised road trip."

"You seen Paul?" she asked.

I shook my head.

"I didn't see him for almost a year. I tried, but he wouldn't. He's a journalist, you know."

"Yeah. Philadelphia, right?"

"Uh-huh. I finally saw him. It was awkward. I tried to talk, but it was clearly the last thing he wanted. We stuck to banalities. Our desperation to ignore the elephant in the room was ridiculous. I invited him to my wedding. He sent a gift but didn't come."

"I wrote, got nothing."

"Talk about revealing yourself," she said. "I can see why he doesn't want to rehash it."

"That was one of the biggest things, his leaving. It was the worst thing, in the long-term. I had known him for years. I was as close to him as I'd been to anyone in my life. And essentially, he pushed us in front of a loaded gun so he could save himself. That stuck. It made all those years of friendship seem meaningless. It meant there was no one, no matter what I'd thought. That I never had him, and if not him, then not you… no one. I wondered, how could I be so wrong about somebody?" I went on, "I looked back for signs that he lied about everything. Signs that you did."

"I don't think he was lying," Louisa said. "He probably disappointed himself as much as he did us. I mean, what could he do? How could he redeem himself? Saying 'I'm sorry,' would have been ridiculous. Would you have forgiven him?"

She was right. I wouldn't have. "But you were willing," I said. "You contacted him, talked to him."

"I don't know," she admitted. "I think I was relieved that he was petulant. It let me off the hook. I didn't have to try anymore." She paused and poked at her pastry for a moment. "Will you try to see him?"

"I have to," I said. "Maybe just to see who he is. I don't know." I leaned back in my chair. "When I saw you come outside, you seemed so much the same, looking exactly and doing exactly what I would have thought."

"Utter predictability," she muttered.

"No. It's just you still being you. And yes, that's a good thing."

She smiled.

"So what do you think of me now?" I asked.

"The same. You're what you always were. You're a romantic. Big. Old school. Die hard."

"Almost did."

"And may again. You'll never learn."

"You have?"

"I was never a romantic. I always knew how to separate my fantasies from the world. You've always tried living yours. I remember that damned saxophone. You still have that?"

"I do," I confessed. "I don't try to play it anymore, though."

"Progress."

"I thought you'd say that I'd changed utterly," I confessed, almost disappointed.

"As usual, you would have been wrong. How are you physically?"

"Okay. Good. A bit of a limp, as you see. I have to admit that vanity kept the cane at the hotel. I use it sometimes to keep it from getting too sore, but I don't have to."

"How tough was the recovery?"

"Lots of physical therapy. But I had my mother's contempt for weakness of any kind to gently nudge me forward."

"How is she?"

"Strangely content. She seems to have accepted my, uh, unorthodox life choices without complaint. They don't affect her, so I guess it doesn't matter. I see her a couple of times a year."

"And what happens now?"

"I'm here for a few days. You take me to meet the folks and show me around. And then, forward."

"Paul?"

"Yeah."

"What about Cindy?"

I shook my head. "Don't think so." Mrs. Gerald had mentioned seeing Cindy, and now Louisa. I began to wonder why I'd never thought of doing it. I vacillated between wondering if I was trying to avoid her and why, and telling myself that she was just a little girl. She'd probably have forgotten most of it anyway. And what good could rifling the poor girl's memories do?

"You know that going back over all of this," Louisa said, "… don't get me wrong. I'm glad you did. I'm glad you're here, but you might be doing it again, living your fantasies, playing the romantic."

"I know," I smiled. "Die hard."

* * *

I felt like a prisoner, hands aloft, walking toward Loewy, Paul's abandonment and Jesse's desire to stop still too much to comprehend.

When we got close enough to see each other, Loewy's face registered a mild horror that morphed into pity. It reflected what he saw in me. I must have looked half-dead. I felt it. I didn't see a way out anymore. This road had been endless. It led nowhere. It was lined with guns.

I wanted to wipe that ghastly look from his face. It was like a mirror with a doomed image of me trapped inside.

To divert his attention, I blurted, "I don't know where he went."

It worked. Once more, he was all about the job. I couldn't stand him looking at me like he gave a damn. It meant that I had to.

"The shots?"

"I don't think it hit him. Jesse couldn't see enough to hit anything."

Loewy looked around as if he might spot Paul in the near distance. "So he's just out there?"

I shrugged. "I guess."

Loewy threw up his hands in exasperation. "What made him run?"

"I don't know," I almost shouted with exasperation. "General dickishness?"

He glared at me. "I don't deserve this shit, and you can't afford it," he murmured, menacing. "Look down there." He pointed at the road. "I got cops climbin' up my ass to get a crack at you, and I'm the only thing standin' in their way. You wanna give up? Fine. I will too." He looked at me, waiting for a response. I said nothing. He started marching for the police line.

"I'm scared!" I hollered. I found myself crying. I could barely talk for it.

Loewy turned around.

"He said 'I don't wanna drive no more.' Just like that. Simple. Like we had choices, like this was a choice. And then Paul just runs. He didn't know what would happen. It could have set Jesse off; he might've shot everyone in the car. But Paul didn't give a shit. Fucking coward saved his own ass, though."

Getting mad helped me gain control.

"Did Jesse say why he wanted to stop?"

"No."

"You think he might be ready to give up, turn himself in?"

"He said he didn't want to drive anymore. That's all. I didn't have a chance to talk to him. Paul ran, and then the shots. You called… I had to come down here. I couldn't talk to him."

"Is he angry or desperate?" Loewy begged. "Is he ready to give up, or ready to die?"

"I don't know!" I yelled. Again, tears, half a guttural scream of frustration. It didn't last long. Hands on hips, I breathed again.

"You okay?"

I nodded.

"You've done a real good job," Loewy said, "keeping it together. I don't think a lot of people could have."

"I could have turned him in. There must have been some way. When Cindy came, I should have found a way to take her back..."

"Why didn't you?"

"It was so fast," I pleaded. "She pops up out of nowhere. It's night. He's got a gun. It was the first thing to do at daylight. It's what we were doing when you found us."

I stopped. I didn't want to go on, but Loewy's silence insisted.

"Both of 'em," I confessed, "they wanted something so bad. I did too. Jesse wanted out of some town. Cindy wanted away from God knows what."

"What did you want?"

I couldn't say it aloud, but the answer I heard was Becca's voice: *You've got wings, brother...* I heard it like she stood right in front of me and I longed to confess to this man, regardless of how foolish it seemed, *I wanted to fly*. Just the thought of doing so made me lose it again. I cried uncontrollably that so pathetic a want had led to this blood-drenched, sickening dread. I cried remembering Becca's face as she'd said it, wondering if she thought she was gifting me with something that I didn't know, or flattering with what she thought I did. I wished I could have blamed it all on her—blamed all the blood and fear on that grandiloquent, fawning farewell.

"For a while," I said, when I'd regained enough control to speak, "I forgot all of it—the noise, the bullshit... jobs, DJ patter... sameness..." I paused, again afraid to acknowledge the truth, but finding the courage this time. "I forgot about people dying."

And then my father's image, a hollow-eyed man begging me to be what he had not. A stunted romantic willing me the benefit of his unlived dreams, as clueless as I was to their consequence.

"For a minute back there," I said, "we were all free."

"Free's scary," Loewy said. "Most don't take much stock in it."

The wind stirred and I felt the chill. Loewy wrapped his coat around him. "Gets cold out here at night," he said. "Nothin' like Boston, though."

Despite my best efforts, more tears rolled down my face. "I'm sorry. Can't keep doing that." I smeared them away. "Gotta keep it together."

"Hey. You're human."

"Can you help us?"

"I'm trying."

"You said Boston. You from Boston?"

"A townie."

He smiled. We both did.

Nothing left to say, I turned back to the car.

XII

An ending seemed at hand. I didn't know what it would be, but this felt like one. Again, I approached the car as if it were a sentence, looked at the huddled figures inside, and recoiled from the reflection of myself I saw in their faces.

"We might as well stretch out some," I said as I opened the passenger door.

Louisa hesitated a moment before she stepped from the car, Cindy in tow. Jesse sat in the back, looking out into the night. I stooped to talk to him. This was my chance to talk him down, I thought. The talk with Loewy had given me strength enough to try.

"Come on," I coaxed, trying to lure him from the car. I hoped that little bit of movement, the small change from inside the car to outside the car would make a difference.

"You all ain't laughin' at me now, huh?" he repeated.

I bowed my head in shame and sadness. He was a child. A child with a gun. So young that mild ridicule remained top-of-mind when he had shot a man two days before.

"Come on, Jesse. You haven't been out of the car in days."

He looked at the cops.

"Just stay low," I assured him.

After a moment, he stepped from the car, creeping low as if ducking artillery fire only he could hear. I motioned Louisa and Cindy back to the car. "You folks get some sleep."

Jesse and I both crabwalked to a rise about 20 feet away. He made sure he could see the car. There we sat. I watched him slip the gun into his jacket pocket. I hoped the hand would emerge without it. I don't know what I would have done if it had. I imagined myself lunging at him, a mighty scuffle in the desert dirt, a popping noise, perhaps one of us dead. Would I have had the guts for that? Or would I have done nothing? It didn't matter. His hand remained in his pocket, the barrel protruding through the thin red fabric.

I listened to the desert sounds, a pulsing hiss, like a heartbeat, punctuated with insect bleeps and animal yowls. I felt Jesse watching me. I stared up at the stars and he down at the ground.

"Why'd you want to stop?" I asked.

He waited so long I didn't think he would answer.

"Just did," he finally said

"We're almost there, you know."

He, too, looked up at the stars. "There are too many," he said.

I assumed he meant the stars. I didn't understand. I didn't ask.

"It's like church," he said. "Like candles. I barely ever went to church when I was a kid."

He looked at me, expectant, as if I would understand.

"You believe in heaven?" he asked me.

I didn't answer. He blinked and tears fell down his face.

"I'm not gonna get there," he said.

"Heaven," I asked lightly, "or California?"

He smiled. "Either."

"Of course you will. You're gonna race Cindy to the water. You said so."

"I could've been different out there, if we'd made it. You and me."

"That cop I'm talking to is a good guy. If I take you to him, no one'll hurt you."

"Look at 'em down there," he said, nodding to the line of cops. "All they have to do is shoot me. Then it's over. Ain't nobody out there waitin' for me. I'll just go away."

"Heaven bound?" I asked.

He shrugged. “Can’t get there from here,” he shyly said, and smiled at that.

He took his eyes from the sky and stared straight at me.

“If I die, bury me out here, huh?”

I could have told him that nobody was going to die, but I was too exhausted to lie.

“It’s beautiful,” I said, looking around us, “even at night when you can’t see it.”

“Yeah,” he replied against the desert’s easy breathing, fleetingly oblivious to the guns, his own and those below. “This is peaceful.”

* * *

“That friend o’ yours didn’t help matters any,” said Loewy, more expressive with his second drink. “We started looking for him after you told me he ran. I sent men out to flank your car and they found him sitting all curled up against the cold about 500 yards east of you. They put him in a squad car. By the time I got there, an FBI guy was sitting in the back seat questioning him. Yeah. The Feds got in on it. I don’t remember the guy’s name. Something with ‘P,’ like ‘Parent’ or ‘Parenna.’ I sat in the front to listen and dared him to say anything about me bein’ there. He gave me the evil eye, but he didn’t say a thing, just went to back work.

“At first your guy wasn’t saying much. What was his name?”

“Paul,” I answered.

“Yeah. FBI kept asking him why he robbed the gas station, if he was the one who shot the cop. Trying to fluster him. Succeeding, too. His head dartin’ from face to face begging someone to save him, mouth open, head shaking ‘no, no, no.’ I wanted to stop it, but I’d pushed it to the limit sitting in without permission. I felt sorry for him, but there was nothing I could do.

“He finally started talkin’ and insisted he didn’t shoot anyone, that the Jesse guy robbed the station, that he was the one with the gun and that he shot the cop.

"'Why'd you kidnap the girl, then?' FBI asked him. By this time, your Paul was practically cryin', slamming his fists on his thighs, sayin' that he didn't shoot nobody and didn't kidnap the girl. I felt a lot better about believing you and handling it like I did. In fact, I piped up, 'That's the same thing my guy says.' And then FBI lights in on you. 'What about him, the driver, what did he have to do with it?' I got worried when I saw the look on your friend's face. It was one of those 'lights on' things. It's what you get when someone's cornered and sees a way out. He calmed down and started doing a lot less denying.

"He said the trip was your idea and that you were the one who took a shine to the gunman. Said he and the girl tried to turn him in at the restaurant. 'Lennie didn't help you?' FBI says, and your guy says, 'No.' Also said that when the little girl showed up, you weren't in any hurry to get her back home. FBI liked that. I think it was sexier, having a rich Harvard boy involved. Made him seem special, like he nabbed a big fish instead of some poor slob sixteen-year-old who got hold of his momma's gun. People believe what they wanna believe. They believe what serves 'em best. In this case, it was you as a bad guy.

"Your boy knew what the Fed wanted to hear. He was like a dog doing tricks for a pat on the head. FBI nodded his head when he said things he liked, then your friend nodded his head in response and kept going, embellishing, little detail here, a little detail there. Said you went off to have private heart-to-hearts with the shooter; said you talked to the little girl about taking her to California."

Talking to Loewy, it made sense. Nothing they believed was a lie. I did have private chats with Jesse. I did talk about California with Cindy. With every childish misjudgment magnified, I looked less the innocent and more like the confederate. I was, in a way. But a part of me screamed, 'No!' that I was not. Especially after I thought Jesse had no bullets. After that, I'd placed a gloss of lightness over the whole thing, but I'd thought the gun was empty. I had seen it and held it. Previously, I admit, I'd minimized him, the boy-man with a gun, and made light of a missing child because they fed my need to paint myself with bigger strokes, in brighter colors. It furthered my attempts to create an extraordinary life.

"By the time they finished talking to your Paul," Loewy continued, "there was a new scenario. Instead of you happening along and getting caught up in this, you were kidnapped at first, but then became a kind of an accomplice. They never outright said that you were responsible, never said you held a gun or forced the girl to do anything, but you stoked the flames. Like with my captain, you were the devil, dancin' around and whispering things in peoples' ears. You pulled the strings, they decided, because you were too smart to do the deeds yourself. The kid was an accident waiting to happen; you made sure it did. I guess that Harvard thing really set a lotta people off.

"From then on, they talked more about you than the kid. They tried to get ahold of your parents, your mother, but they couldn't. Someone said she was out of the country. They asked your friend if he could talk you into giving up. That's how far it had gone; they'd moved past the kid with the gun. Now you were the perp; getting at you would end it. Your friend said there was nothing he could do. He asked to leave. I thought that was strange. Thought he'd want to stick around and make sure everyone was okay. They asked him again to talk with you, but I remember it to this day: 'He won't listen to me,' he said. 'No one's said "no" to him in his life.' He just sat there for a moment. Then, as he was getting up to go he said, 'A rich boy…' as if that explained it all.

"He got in a car, and they drove him away. I never saw him again."

* * *

After what I'd heard from Loewy and Louisa, I spent two days in Philadelphia before I screwed up the courage to visit the *Inquirer* offices where Paul worked. I had not called ahead; I knew he'd refuse to see me. At the inevitability of confronting him, my bitterness grew. It surprised me. I didn't realize how much energy I'd spent shoving it away.

There I was, standing in the newspaper lobby, jiggling my foot impatiently and staring out the floor-to-ceiling windows at the determined-looking folk striding in and out, their half-earned self-righteousness etched upon their 'defenders-of-the-truth' journalistic faces… sitting there—when it was far too late—and only now asking myself what I wanted from the meeting. I got bad answers: an apology, an acknowledgment, a plea for forgiveness, tearful rapprochement. The odds were excellent that I'd get none of them. So what did I want? What was the point of being here?

I knew that Paul might have been an excuse—a convenient target for my anger, giving me someone besides myself to blame. He hadn't caused the outcome. But he'd helped it along. He had betrayed me, violated my trust and friendship. It was like I'd come home to find that he'd ransacked my house, smeared shit on the paintings and the furniture, broken every pane of glass. I wanted to know why. I wanted to face the one who'd done that to me and ask why.

So I sat on a sofa in the lobby and waited. I had asked the security guard to ding me when he came in. I lied that I had information for a story Paul was working on. After about 20 minutes, the guard waved. He motioned to Paul and spoke to him, pointing me out. I stood up as Paul looked over. Unlike Louisa, he did not look the same. He looked surprisingly different. There was nothing in that face of the boy I knew in college.

His face went blank, and I watched his expression curdle. It morphed from the journalist's home turf assuredness to shock, then anger. He glared at me with the buried hurt reserved for someone who'd stolen something precious from him.

"Paul," I said, conscious of my attempt to smile and sound welcoming. It did feel good somehow to see him. My resentment slipped. I saw the kid who'd been my good friend.

He didn't move. He stared at me, the hurt and anger still printed on his face. He stood frozen, like he didn't know what to do or say. Maybe too many clashing urges all at once.

"Can I talk to you?" I asked.

His head twitched and as if that tiny movement freed him, he gestured toward the couch in invitation and sat in an adjacent chair. He sat on the very edge of the seat, elbows on knees and hands clasped before him. He watched his folded hands for a moment and then he looked at me, waiting.

"How are you?" I lamely began.

Something between a shiver and a shrug acknowledged the question's limpness.

"Fine, Lennie. What can I do for you?"

"I wanted to see you, Paul. I saw Louisa. She said that you guys hadn't talked for a long time."

"You here to chide me for poor social skills?" he snarked.

I had to smile. The comment was vintage Paul.

"What's funny?" he asked, offended.

"Just that that was so you… so much the you I remember."

He did not return the smile. "What do you want, Lennie?"

"I'm sorry," I said, apologizing for forgetting what had happened, for thinking him a friend again. "I'm talking to people who were there. Like I said, I saw Louisa, Cindy's mother even, and I'm trying to… put it all together. See it how other people saw it. Trying to understand."

He was staring at his hands again. I waited. He said nothing.

"I want to get past it," I continued a little more desperately. "Maybe I want to stop thinking about it. Maybe I want absolution. Maybe…"

"That you don't get," he interrupted. He was looking at me now. "Not from me."

I nodded. "I put it all in motion, I know. I'm to blame. I know that and I'm sorry, but there could have been a thousand other outcomes. I think I know why I did what I did, but I don't know about anyone else. That's what this is about."

"That's a start. You thinking about somebody else."

I ignored the dig. I didn't even care if I deserved it. I had to know about him.

"I wanted to know why you left us," I said.

His mouth fell open and he leaned back in awe. "I didn't leave '*us*'," he cried. "I left *you*."

"Why?"

"Because you dragged me into a situation that could have got me killed. You took a fancy to some sicko with a gun and decided he was harmless and risked all of our lives. You ignored everything I told you and did as you pleased and to hell with everyone else. I left *you*."

"What about Cindy and Louisa?"

He looked abashed for an instant. "Cindy wasn't my problem," he said, his eyes back on his hands. "She should've been at the nearest police station as soon as we found her. Louisa made up her own mind. She could've done the same."

"You know I didn't mean for any of that to happen," I told him. "You must know how sorry I am that it did."

"My God!" He shook his head in exasperation. "You hooked up with some sick kid and then kidnapped a little girl, but you didn't *mean* it...?"

"You were there, Paul," I replied. "It's not that simple. You know it. You know that."

"I know I was lucky to get out alive. I almost got killed because of you. Now you come here asking forgiveness and a trip down nightmare lane?"

"You were my best friend," I replied.

"I was young."

"You didn't know what would happen, how it would affect Jesse, what would happen to any of us. You could have gotten everyone killed, too."

"I didn't owe you staying. You didn't deserve it."

"Louisa and Cindy, did they deserve it?"

Silence.

"We're picking right up from our last conversation, aren't we?" He looked surprised and almost amused at the irony.

It was my turn to stare at my hands. In college, we had shared every lust and longing and silly ideal. I could barely believe that this was the same person, yet it made perfect sense that this was the person he'd become. I wondered if I seemed as foreign and familiar a creature to him as he did to me.

"You were my friend," I said, apropos of nothing.

He stood. "Forgiveness denied," he announced. "We done?"

"You don't even look the same," I said, marveling at the changes in him.

He turned away.

"Sometimes, Paul," I called, limping behind him, "shit just happens. Things go wrong. Things you'd never expect."

He faced me once he'd pushed the elevator button. "We had no business out there," he said with all sincerity, almost pleading, as if trying to convince me and unable to believe I didn't understand. "We didn't belong. You were the only reason we were out there. If it weren't for you, we wouldn't have been and it never would have happened."

And then I finally realized what this was about. "And you never would have run," I said. He would not have live with an ugly piece of himself that most would never have to see.

"I am so sorry, Paul," I said, exhibiting too much of the pity I felt for him then.

His face curdled. "Everything you got, you deserved," he spat. He stared past me as he disappeared behind the elevator doors.

* * *

"It's not blue like you might think."

Jesse and I sat on the rise overlooking the car and the darting of flashlight beams from the police lines beyond.

"The ocean's more green than blue," I continued, "and if you find an empty place, you can sit out on the sand and see only water and hear only the waves' rise and fall, and you can imagine it goes on forever."

Jesse stared at the desert night as if the ocean lay there and he heard its ragged swayings.

"What should I do?" he asked.

I bowed my head with relief. It was the opening I'd prayed for. "We need to let Cindy and Louisa go," I said. "Then I'll take you to meet the guy I've been talking to. He won't hurt you. You'll be okay. We can end it."

He thought a moment, and nodded assent. "Tomorrow," he said, staring at his imaginary ocean. "Tomorrow."

"You like the sunrise?" I asked.

He nodded.

"Dawn, then."

He looked at the sky. "A lotta stars," he said.

"You can see more of 'em out here, without artificial lights from buildings and streetlamps."

"How come no one lives out here?" he asked.

"I guess it's too far from people."

"I like that," he said.

"Me too."

I felt calm and present for the first time in days. I didn't have to hide in a reverie somewhere. I thought of what Jesse would go through once arrested and jailed and made a promise to myself to help him, hire him a lawyer, do what I could. He was alone. He exuded it like scent.

"Whose blood was that?" he asked.

He had never alluded to the shooting. I didn't want to scare him with the truth of it.

"Someone got hit."

"Is he dead?"

"I don't know."

From the look he gave, he knew I was lying.

"Let's go back to the car. Get some rest," I coaxed.

He didn't move. After a moment, I touched his arm. "Come on." As I rose, so did he. We crouched our way back to the car. I put my finger to my lips to signal quiet; Louisa and Cindy slept in the front. I slipped into the back seat and he followed. I'd never known such bone weariness, my eyelids like lead. It took everything to keep them open. I leaned my head back and trembled from the cold. I felt a nudge and opened my eyes to see Jesse holding out his jacket.

"Aren't you cold?" I asked him.

"No. Go on."

"Thanks." I slipped it on. Drowsily, I reached out and touched his arm. "Thank you," I repeated as I fell asleep.

My eyes opened before the faintest light on the skyline. Jesse slept with his head on my shoulder. It surprised me, but seemed surprisingly natural. He was a scared, lonely boy after all. I was a scared, lonely boy after all. Right then, our connection was physical and unambiguous. I felt his breath on my neck, his hair against my face. I could smell him, and I wanted to protect him like I would a sleeping child.

No movement in the front seat; Louisa and Cindy slept as well. I felt safe. The sunrise fire poking through the night promised something spectacular. With three sleeping bodies around me, inside the car, watching the sun come up, for some reason, I felt safe. I hadn't paid attention to a sunrise in a long while.

Then I remembered the gun. I felt the jacket pocket. It wasn't there. Jesse still slept soundly. Gently, I slipped his head from my shoulder. He didn't wake. I leaned forward enough to tap Louisa. She started. I quickly shushed her.

"Take Cindy and go," I told her. Shoving back sleep she leaned over Cindy and whispered. She silently unlatched the door and swung it open. Cindy scrambled out first, and Louisa followed. I wanted to call Loewy and warn him they were coming, but the radio would have woken Jesse. Outside, Louisa beckoned. "Come on," she whispered. I looked at Jesse sleeping in the seat next to me and shook my head 'no.' This way, if he woke up, there'd be someone there, and he wouldn't go after them. I wasn't going to leave him; I'd promised. With hand gestures, I pushed her away. She slipped the door almost shut and disappeared.

* * *

"I'm sitting there half dozing," Loewy said, "when someone says two people are heading from the car—the girl and the kid. If you'd been there, I woulda kissed you. I knew you did it. Yes! I went to look, and they were coming down, big as life and looking unharmed, didn't even look that scared. I'm celebratin' inside and realize I don't see FBI, so I head back to his car. He's giving orders. I listen and realize he's giving orders for takin' down the car. The kid was free, so it was safe, he said, and the light would hit the car in a few minutes. We'd be able to see in. You'd parked in just the right place. You wouldn't see us, but we could see you. He'd give you a chance to come out, but then he'd go in. I told him, 'What if I'm right and you're wrong?' What if you were clean in all this? Didn't matter. He said it outright: your friend Paul had given him enough to cover his ass no matter what happened to you.

"I begged them to let me go up and talk to you one more time. They wouldn't. Said it ended then."

I sat in Loewy's living room with elbows on my knees. My forehead rested on my folded hands. The grain pattern in the hardwood floor swerved and flowed like liquid, ending in whirled knots and starting up again. It was rude, not looking at him. I didn't mean to be, but all of this was new. Seeing the parts converge—my actions, leading to theirs, leading to someone else's—for the first time, I saw the finished whole. As he spoke, Loewy was both more and less than a person; he was sound and memory—he was history. I listened to him like I would an audiobook. Sometimes I closed my eyes and saw the scene described, even saw the car in which I sat, saw it as if from the police line, parked on the rise, the object of fretful attention.

"I am sorry," Loewy said.

My head jerked up at the strange interruption. I was afraid I had missed something. "This is hard for you." He scooted forward in his chair. "I didn't realize it would be. I guess I could've been a little more delicate."

"Not a problem," I replied. "It's what I need to hear."

He rose from his seat and placed his hand on my head, displaying the tenderness that made me trust him ten years ago. When his hand touched the scar, I jerked away. "I'm sorry," I blurted, hands raised in innocence and apology. I hadn't meant to do that.

He sat back down and looked at me long enough and with enough sympathy that I averted my eyes. I never knew why someone caring always made pain that much more raw, but it did. Sometimes the worst thing you can do to someone is care.

"I tell myself I did everything I could," he said. "But that doesn't stop me from realizing I could have done things different, or better. You and I, we had sort of a pact. You kept your end, and I didn't keep mine. I meant to keep you safe. When I first met you, I walked away thinking, 'No one has to get hurt in this.' Because I trusted you. I truly thought you'd come through, and you did. You kept up your end. I let mine fall.

"They bundled your friend—the girl—they bundled her off somewhere the minute she arrived, but when she heard the shot and all the commotion, she ran. People were scramblin' everywhere. She saw your car moving and tore after it like she could grab it and stop it with her bare hands. Then she stopped and her hands flew to her face. People caught up with her. I wasn't one of the first, but from where I was, I heard her screaming, 'It's him! It's him!' as she pointed at the car. I knew she meant you. I looked around for FBI but couldn't find him. I saw the unmarked cars chasing after yours. I jumped in a squad car and told the uniform to drive. Your friend, she popped out o' nowhere, pounding on the car. The look on her face, I didn't even have to think. I knew what she wanted. I opened the door as the little girl screamed her name, I mean screamed it, like for her life. Her parents stood there holding her back, but she broke free and ran. Your friend jumped in the car and right behind her, the little girl. I was cussin' under my breath, but nothin' to do but take off. Like it was habit, the girl jumped on your friend's lap and held onto her. They both looked terrified. On the radio, I heard it. They said the shooter was driving. Your friend grabbed my arm and she was shakin' her head, but she didn't say anything. I heard 'em say they had a clean shot. She dug her nails in my arm and it was like she couldn't speak, like she was rigid, but she kept shaking her head.

"She said, 'It's him.' She talked like her mouth barely worked and it was hard to form the words. 'It's him!'"

* * *

I sat next to Jesse in the back seat, perfectly still, long enough for Louisa and Cindy to reach safe distance. As I sat, I felt his heartbeat against my side as the sun began to rise. On the vast, empty desert floor, I imagined the earth struggling, groaning as if on a rusty axle to point this place toward the sun. I gently nudged Jesse and pointed at the horizon. He wiped his eyes, his face impassive as he took it in. Like a puppy ignorant of personal space, he clambered over me to see more. He didn't say anything, but he looked out of the car as if at a movie screen. The sunrise was beautiful in this barren place.

When it seemed most intense, with the first hints of the sun's light and heat, when its rays colored the long, wispy clouds with an artist's palette of heavy colors, he sat back in his seat. He turned to me.

"Bury me out here," he said.

I barely glimpsed the dark gray barrel at his chin before the blood and bone splattered my face. The blinding noise burnt my ears, my head. The blood-smeared windshield shattered. His head flew back, and I reached for it. I grabbed his shirt and pulled him up. His mouth was moving, making sounds. I heard screaming. I tried to wipe the blood from his face. I wiped and wiped, but barely saw skin or hair or anything of him as more blood covered it. I wished the screaming would stop. My hand touched a jagged edge of bone at the top of his head and sunk inside. I pushed it away, but his hand reached out to me. Everything I saw turned red, a red film over my eyes. The screaming got louder and I slipped and slid in blood as I scrambled over the front seat and landed behind the wheel. I turned the key and stomped on the pedal. The car sped and bounced over the rough terrain. The screaming wouldn't stop. Metal and flashing lights came from all directions. His hand touched my head. I let go of the wheel. My arms struck out like I was slapping at bees. The screaming never stopped until the unbearable sting, like a high-pitched note, sliced through my head, silencing everything.

* * *

"It was you," Loewy said. "I got it; she was saying that it was you behind the wheel. I almost choked. I grabbed the radio, but I was talking before I even pushed the button. I fumbled with the handset and just kept screaming, 'It's not him! It's not the shooter!' I don't even know if I ever pushed the button. They said they never heard me. There was too much chatter. I drove faster, almost rolled over trying to drive on the dirt. Didn't know what I was gonna do, but I had to get to you."

* * *

Everything slowed as the high-pitched note shrieked louder. I felt my body slow, drift in slow motion. My face fell; my arms fell; the world outside the windshield grew blinding with light as my head hit the seat and my limbs flew in all directions, like I was weightless and some force shook the car that held me. I tried to crawl, and I remember trying to hold onto something, desperately, like I had to hold on and crawl into it to survive. And then it worked: I got inside and it felt warm and it held me tight. That's the last thing I remember.

* * *

"I saw the car slow down, slow down, slow down. It took forever for it to stop, like it was drifting. The police cars caught up and surrounded it. Men jumped out, guns drawn. The driver's door flew open and you stumbled out. You were covered with blood. Your head was covered in blood. They were yelling at you to get on the ground. It was stupid. They were reciting lines from the police manual, and you were stumbling around blind and bloody. I slammed my brake and ran for it. They were yelling louder and louder and I knew you couldn't hear 'em. I hadn't heard the shot, but I knew what happened. They saw me running, and from the corner of my eye, I saw their guns turn my way. They were so amped, they almost shot at me, but I held out my arm like my palm would stop bullets and kept going. I got to you and I saw your head and you were moaning, crying, trying to talk but I couldn't understand you. You were reaching out and I was trying to hold you still. It was like I was fighting with you, trying to force you down, stop you moving. I couldn't help you if you wouldn't stop moving. I thought you'd die if you didn't stop. Finally, I shoved your arms down and put mine around all of you. I started sinking to the ground and forced you down with me. I screamed for someone to help me. They all stood around pointing their goddamned guns like someone was gonna jump up and pounce on 'em. 'Goddammit, help me!' I screamed. One of 'em came over. We held you down and then you went still. I tapped your face, trying to wake you up. I called your name, but nothing. The cop called out for the paramedic. I was still calling your name when he got there and pushed me away.

"I asked the paramedic if you were alive, but he didn't answer. I yelled it, and he said, 'Yes.'

"I looked in the car and saw the shooter, bloody on the floor in the back. I could tell he was dead, but I felt for a pulse. There was none. I looked at him and thought that you were right. He was a kid. They put you on a stretcher, and only then, I saw the jacket you had on, the one the shooter wore. They told us the shooter wore a red jacket. That's all we knew about him. That's why they thought you were him. They shot you because you were wearing his red jacket."

I hadn't known. I remembered very little of what happened after Jesse shot himself. "You saved my life," I said, studying Loewy's kind face. It was hard to fathom. I could not have imagined the gratitude, the pure affection I felt toward him right then. It surprised me how visceral it was. Right then, I knew what it meant—the bond you feel with someone who saved your life.

"Barely," he replied. "I should've done better."

Looking at him, the man to whom I owed my life, I saw my father, blaming himself for a job well-done that still didn't rate. I wasn't sure if my tears were for Loewy, myself, or my father. Maybe all three of us. I don't know who he saw in me, but Loewy lowered his head and struggled with tears as well. He rose and I stood and he put his arms around me. He laid his hand on the back of my neck, a gesture I knew from my father, acknowledging his power and his duty to protect me forever, no matter the cost—a duty my father had helplessly shirked, and one that Loewy had taken on himself for some godforsaken reason and feared he'd failed. Loewy half whispered, "It's all right."

I hugged him back, hard, and for that moment felt my father's arms again. "Thank you," I said.

"Seeing you today, I'll accept that. I thought I did it all wrong for a long time. I'm glad you showed yourself to me—whole."

Ever since then (I didn't know what to call it—the 'event,' the 'episode,' nothing sounded right, either too vague or too melodramatic, self-aggrandizing or full of denial) I'd been broken. The limp was just the outward sign. It was in talking with Loewy that I began to think I might get whole again—different, never the same, but maybe whole.

"It's your fault I'm still here," I smiled.

"I'm sorry about the young one," he said, "but the way things went down, there wasn't much of a chance for him."

I more than toyed with the idea of fate, so maybe it went both ways. It could hold you in reserve for a place at the mountaintop, or dangle your feet just above unbearable pain with a promise of nothing different, nothing more.

"Never was much for him," I replied.

* * *

We talked for hours, graduating to mundanities—his neighborhood, his hobbies. I left him that day with another hug and a promise, which we kept. We stayed in touch. He sent me photos of his grandkids as they grew. I kept him up to date on my foals and rescues. It was always a pleasure to hear from him. He used to call to make sure I got the emails he sent from the computer his kids had given him one Christmas and which he never learned to trust.

He got ill three years ago. He died soon after. I wanted to go to visit him, but he asked me not to. He said he didn't want to say goodbye. We parted a couple of times, but we never said goodbye.

He was a good man. I have missed him. He was the last of my protectors.

XIII

Louisa and I sat in her living room, watching her five-year-old purposefully build a castle out of wooden blocks in the middle of the floor. A sweet child, he looked remarkably like her as he furrowed his brow, examining one block versus another to determine which would properly expand the elaborately jagged form before him.

"I have never been so deliberative about anything," I told Louisa as we watched the child approach the task as if it were surgery.

"That's me," she said. "Quite the schoolmarm."

She looked at my cane. It was old and subtly carved. If I was going to use one, I figured it might as well be stylish.

"Nineteenth century," I told her. "Found it at an antique store not long after I left rehab."

"How long did the therapy take?" she asked.

"Three months inside. Another six months, three times a week. Only because I could afford it. If I weren't rich, I wouldn't have an occasionally annoying limp; I'd probably be shuffling. Considering a bullet to the head, I guess a leg is getting off easy."

I finished telling her about my meeting with Loewy, how I hadn't expected how deeply he'd held the memory… the weight it bore within him.

"It surprised me how much we seemed—at least for the time we spoke—how much we seemed to mean to each other. I didn't know what he'd done for me."

"I only sat and watched," she said, her eyes on her child. When she turned to me, they were full of shame. "I never left the car. You fell out of the car, and I couldn't even recognize you. It wasn't you. It was some bloody thing lurching around like a movie monster. I couldn't talk; I couldn't move. I remember Cindy grabbing onto me so hard it hurt. I just watched."

I touched her hand. "It's okay," I said, sad that she rebuked herself for anything. She had nothing to be sorry for.

"I thought I would have been more heroic," she said with a smile. "I had thought myself more of a pioneer woman than that. Illusion shattered; it proved me just a suburban girl."

We watched the boy in silence for a while.

"I often wish," she said, "to this day that I were more like you."

"Gimpy?"

"No," she replied. "A bit grand."

I squeezed her hand. "Grandly foolish is more like it."

She wiggled her hand in a 'maybe, maybe not' gesture. "Even if that's part of it, it doesn't change the fact. It makes sense that you moved out there. You need a bigger canvas."

"I raise horses," I countered. "Hardly grand."

"Doesn't matter. All the better, in fact. It's not what you do. You know that. It's about how much living you're willing to face, how much death. For me, that's not very much. I have a big city and a small canvas here. I get lonely outside my crowded cocoon. It's scary out there. You can face it. I can't."

"I have no choice," I said.

"I know."

We talked until sunset about all kinds of things. Her husband came home and we all had dinner. She was right. He seemed a kind man. It also seemed clear that he loved her dearly. He may not have been her grand passion, but she was his.

About to climb into my cab, I asked her the question I'd been avoiding, "Did you ever hear from Cindy, afterwards?"

"I was wondering when you'd get back to that," she said. "I'm impressed that you saved it 'til the cab was driving away."

I bowed my head in deference to the admonition. "Did you talk to her afterwards?" I repeated.

"Yes. Often. Still do." Louisa said.

A thousand questions raced through my head. Did Cindy blame me? Who was she now? I wanted to know that she was okay—that I had done no harm. I wanted assurance of that, and knew Louisa wouldn't give it to me—probably because it wasn't true.

At first, I asked none of my questions. I didn't think I had the right.

"With luck and time, forgotten?" I asked rhetorically.

"My God you can be an ass," she replied.

I truly didn't know what she meant, and looked it.

"Emotional cowardice is no more attractive than any other," she intoned, the headmistress in her ablaze.

My bewilderment increased. I felt like a sitcom husband being accused of something I had no clue about.

With feminine contempt she pulled a piece of paper from her pocket and handed it to me. "I told her you're here," she said. "Do what you will."

I looked at the paper. It was an address in a place called Riverside. I knew it had to be Cindy's address. I looked at Louisa, wondering why she would give this to me, as if she'd done a hurtful thing, both to me and to Cindy. And then I realized what she'd meant by "emotional cowardice." I had never planned to see Cindy; I'd barely even considered it. My first excuses were rational: she had been a child and could add nothing to the factual narrative. But Louisa was a good teacher who chose her words well. I quickly realized that facts weren't the reason for seeing her. It would be personal. Purely personal. Entirely nostalgic. Wholly emotional. That's why I feared it. Beyond facts, it would be about me and the little girl—a grown woman now—whose life I had touched or changed or helped to break.

Louisa watched my wheels turn. "There now," she mocked. "That wasn't so hard." She smiled. "You *have* changed. The old you would never have figured it out."

"I had planned to see Paul next."

"That's easy. Do the hardest part first."

"Coward, huh?"

"A very daring one, but yes."

I guess my whole body signaled resignation. At that, she hugged me. We both held on a long time. I had forgotten how much she meant to me.

"My God, Lennie," she said with bittersweet recognition. "You might be growing up."

We parted tearfully that day. She has always understood me and loved me anyway. I treasure her for that.

* * *

I handed the cabbie the address. He told me to rent a car because it would cost almost two hundred dollars for him to take me. I decided to be rich and spare myself the hassle of a car rental; I said I didn't care.

I wasn't very thoughtful on the mind-numbing drive down endless freeways. Thinking back, I didn't consider who Cindy might have become, or the reception I might get. In fact, I almost fell asleep in the cab.

Alerted as we exited the freeway, we soon stopped in a modest neighborhood, large trash cans out on the curb, either early for the pick up or late to be returned to driveways.

As we stopped, I checked the street address against Louisa's note. This was it. I paid the cabbie and grabbed up my bag. Standing on the sidewalk as the cab drove off, I realized I was in the middle of God knows where with no idea what to expect. I walked up the little sidewalk to the door, which opened. A young girl stood there, tousled light brown hair with blondish streaks in it, light-colored jeans and a loose T-shirt. Her face looked older than I would have expected. Nothing to do with lines or outward signs of age, but in its manner. She impressed less as a girl and more as a woman than I expected of a twenty-year-old.

"You're here," she said, with a note of surprise.

"Louisa didn't tell you? I'm sorry. I thought she had."

"No, I knew. Just… strange," she said, shaking her head. "Come in."

I watched as she scurried to move a cup and saucer from a coffee table. She disappeared and I heard her dump them in a sink. I didn't look at the room. I looked after her, waiting for her, and when she returned, still not having met my eyes, I said, "Cindy?"

For the first time she stopped moving.

"Yeah," she said. She wiped her hand on her jeans and held it out to shake. I dropped my bag and took it. Our eyes locked. From doing everything she could to avoid looking at me, she now held my gaze.

"You remember me?" I stupidly asked.

"Yes. Of course."

"Do you mind that I'm here?

She shook her head and pointed to a chair. She sat in one opposite.

I felt the most disconcerting sense of intimacy with her. I could recognize her. I saw the progression from the little girl to this woman. I sensed I knew her, while knowing that, in fact, I didn't.

"You're hurt?" she asked, noting the limp.

"It's from back then. The trip," I said. I thoughtlessly pointed a finger at my head.

"I'm sorry," she offered. She straightened in her seat. She smiled bravely at me. Then her eyes welled up. She grabbed a tissue and wiped them. She tried the smile again, as if trying to convince me the tears weren't there.

I felt the utter fool. I couldn't believe I had mimed a gun to my head. I watched the first sob shake her, and then she dropped her face into her hand and wept openly. Without thinking, I moved to sit beside her, and put my arm around her.

"My God, I'm ten again," she laughed through tears.

She tried to compose herself, and she couldn't. "I thought you were dead," she wept," when you fell out of the car, all the blood."

"Ssshhh. Ssshhh. You're not supposed to remember," I said, rocking her slowly. "You're supposed to forget."

She leaned her head against me until she gathered herself. Once she'd quieted, she sat upright. "I remember everything," she said, smiling with wet eyes. "I couldn't forget."

As if embarrassed again, her eyes left mine and darted around the room. "Can I get you anything?" she asked, wiping the last of her tears and moving to stand.

"Hold on," I said, taking her hand and pulling her back to her seat. It was strange looking into her twenty-year-old eyes. Back then, she was ten and I was twenty-one. A world separated us. Now, at twenty and thirty-one, respectively, she wasn't that much younger than me, but I still saw the past in her—the child I knew.

"I have to tell you," I said, "how sorry I am that you got caught up in it. I am so sorry."

She drew back, as if stung. "I chose it," she said emphatically. "It wasn't you."

"I talked to your mother."

"She told me. She said you weren't gonna see me. Said you didn't need to."

"I was wrong. I'm sorry I said that. It was me being a coward."

"What kind of bravery did it take?" she asked, clearly hurt.

"I was afraid the whole thing had hurt you, badly, and it was my fault."

"Like I said, it wasn't you. I ran away. I was a little girl."

"Your mother told me about the family back then."

"It wasn't just that. It wasn't just them fighting. It was but it wasn't. It all felt so locked down. They acted like I was deaf or stupid, like I couldn't hear a word. My father saying everything was fine and her saying it was all wrong. To them it was all one thing or another and neither of 'em made any sense to me. They each wanted me on their side and I didn't even know what the sides were. I didn't care. They were just so locked down and everything so hard and tight, like there was a narrow path for each of them and I had to wriggle through one or the other, no other choice."

She looked at me again. "You all seemed so free somehow. I watched you get out of your car. The way you moved, the looks on your faces. It made so much more sense to me. I wanted to be free like that. Even the way Jesse seemed sad made sense to me."

She remembered his name. That struck me.

"The way we looked," I repeated, half-chuckling. "That must have been Harvardian assurance peeking through."

"Whatever it was, I wanted it. Still do."

I took her hand, and I don't know what made me think I had the right, but she didn't object. "What am I to you?" I asked her. "What is that time to you?"

"You were the leader," she said. "You tried to keep us safe. I think you even wanted us to be happy." She slowly pulled her hands away from mine. "I was happy with you all."

I felt so ashamed.

She folded her arms tightly across her chest. "Then I got scared," she said. "Then it was horrible. It all fell down."

She bounded from the sofa. "I'll get you some tea," she announced and disappeared into the kitchen.

I waited for a long time. I noticed a UC Riverside college course book on a table. Also there, a copy of *People* magazine. The place looked like the lair of a poor twenty-year-old who tried. Family photo collections on the wall said she probably had a roommate. There was little indication of who she was, the kind of person she had become, or might. It was all pretty generic.

She finally returned, far more composed, with two cups of tea. "What are you doing now?" I asked as she set them down. "Are you a student?"

"Workin'. Just a job." She nodded toward the course book. "I'm thinking about it. Louisa says I should, but I don't know."

"Why not?" I asked.

"Money. Brains."

"It's clear enough you have the latter."

"I was no ace student. Louisa keeps telling me I should do it."

"She's right."

"For folks like you. Not me. I saw my parents. My mother. Sometimes it's the trying too hard that gets you into trouble."

That sounded as much a lesson she could have learned from me.

"Is that what you were doing when you hid in our car, trying too hard?"

She half-shrugged. "Yeah. Wanting what I couldn't have."

"What was that?" I asked her.

She thought a moment, as if deciding whether or not to say it. "Something different. Something rosy at the end," she said.

We sat in quiet for a while.

"Does it hurt much?" she asked, indicating my leg.

"Not much," I replied. "Sometimes headaches."

She sipped her tea. "Why did he do it?" she asked of her cup.

I didn't know how to answer. How do you tell a young woman that a boy her ten-year-old self cared for couldn't face living anymore?

"It was too hard for him," I said. "He didn't see a way out."

"Nothing better out there," she added, a little too knowingly. "I thought he wanted to see the ocean. I really thought we'd do that. He said he'd race me to it. I imagined that: me and him kicking up sand to get to the waves. I actually dreamed about it the last night."

"He did want it," I replied. "It just wasn't enough."

"What is?"

She looked at me now with earnest inquiry. The question was worrying, but studying her, there was no desperation in it, nothing alarming. She had seen too much blood, and saw death too soon, and she was bright enough to understand what they meant, that's all.

"That's up to you," I told her, "what makes it all right, worth it."

She stood and looked out the window at the small houses in mild states of disrepair. "You come by the freeway?"

"Yeah."

"Freeways remind me of it. It's all flat around here and they go on and on, the same stores and fast food on either side, turning here and there to lead to more places that look just like this one."

"There's better, but you have to find it. And if you do, you might wind up, God knows… with a lost boy with a gun, or a little girl running from something."

She smiled at my small joke.

"And the boy might shoot someone, or himself," she continued, matter-of-fact, her smile fading. "And you might limp for the rest of your life, and have headaches and too much that's… you don't want to remember."

"That's the price you pay."

"It isn't fair."

"Who gives a shit what's fair? Decide what you want to see and go find it." I started sounding pissed and didn't know why. "Whatever the cost. If you're scared you've got wings," I almost shouted at her, "and it's scary… to think you're fucking special, if you're scared of that, you fly!"

She looked disturbed by the very concept. "And fall?" she marveled.

"Yes!" I hissed at her. "Fall."

It was the second time in my life my own words had betrayed me. My telltale tremor returned. I calmed myself, and I repeated, with less heat, watching my hand shake, "You may fall."

She watched me watch my hand as the tremor slowly disappeared.

At first I mistook the look on her face for pity, but it wasn't. It was a combination of fear, compassion, and even a doubtful admiration I didn't deserve.

"What would you do different?" she asked.

I had never allowed myself the luxury of asking. There were too many 'shoulds' and too many alluringly acceptable answers. I thought about it now, sitting there. I ran through the highlight reel and considered all the hell I'd seen. When the answer showed itself, I pondered the lies I might tell that would reflect more kindly on me. Instead, ashamed, I told the truth.

"Nothing," I confessed. I truly didn't know. I hadn't wanted to.

Cindy came over to me. She laid her hand rather kindly, even forgivingly, I thought, on my shoulder.

"You?" I asked her.

She gently kneaded my shoulder, as if in apology. "Everything," she said.

I leaned my head against her and we sat there for a while, a tableau of guilt and acquiescence.

* * *

After the bitter taste of seeing Paul, sitting at the Philadelphia airport, I couldn't go home. I wasn't done yet. I found an Internet station where I pulled up a US map. After examining it, I changed my ticket. I knew Jesse had lived in Western Oklahoma, so I flew to Oklahoma City.

I landed and asked a cabbie to take me to the nearest police station. There, I confused the desk personnel with questions about a ten year-old crime that wasn't even committed on their turf. Fortunately, the questions were bizarre enough that they piqued some interest. There was an older man who vaguely recalled. After a couple of quick phone calls, he told me that Jesse Ahearn had lived in a small town about 60 miles northwest of there. His last name was Ahearn. I had never known that.

I rented a car and drove to Jesse's hometown. The first stop was the local sheriff's office. Again, someone in the office remembered. His mother was long gone, they said, but there was only one cemetery in town. On the way there, I stopped at a gas station store, bought a small something and had them put it in a big bag—which was what I really wanted.

There wasn't much left to the place—the town or the cemetery. Whatever folks used to do for a living wasn't done anymore, or someone in some far off country did it for less. It must have been agonizing. The dilapidated buildings practically moaned with the effort of dying slow. I wondered how many others ran, like Jesse, and I wondered how many got away. Too few, I thought. It wasn't just the buildings; it was the people, their ghosts, like the ghosts Janice carried with her. I wondered if, somewhere, she took solace in knowing that those who'd bred her demons had succumbed to those that someone else created, how those who had wielded such vicious power had been reduced to rubble.

Knee-deep weeds obscured the headstones. Many were simple plaques, flat on the ground. I had to get on my hands and knees and pull the weeds to read them. *Hello, Hannah,* I thought, on seeing a name, *is death what you expected? Hi, Josh. Do you remember? William, are you missed?*

I couldn't find it on the first pass, so I scoured the whole place again. It had to be there. Knees black and muddy, hands chipped and sliced from rocks and weeds, I found it. It only had his name and dates. No "Beloved Son," or anything like that. I doubt he was anyone's beloved.

I hadn't brought a trowel or so much as a spoon, so I used a rock to loosen the dirt. Like a dog, I dug as deep down as I could get. I scooped up handfuls until my bag was half full. I tried to clean up, level out the ground so that I didn't leave a big hole. I also finished pulling up the weeds all around so that his prospect was clear. He had stared at stars and sunrises.

* * *

Nothing had changed. The same majestic pillars jutted from the earth. The same high-pitched chatter annoyed the night. I stayed at a hotel near Monument Valley, watching the tourists innocently gape, loading kids into campers and minivans for the next attraction. They had no idea what lived out here. They didn't know that to the music of its sunrise, a guilty and innocent boy had killed himself. They didn't know that a black woman wandered here, watching them like a ghost and haunted by ghosts of people frightfully like them. They didn't know that out here, a young man's dreams of flight had died.

In my rented four-wheel-drive, I traveled through the desert again, only this time there wasn't the surprise of ten years prior. It was much more like home. Its menace and majesty were as familiar as its prickly brush. I lived in it now. The desert and I—this world and I—had sealed blood oaths.

I got as close to where it happened as I could. I think I remembered. Not exactly, but I got a directional sense that I trusted somehow. I couldn't be sure, but I followed my gut. When I hit the spot that seemed right, I stopped the car. I killed the engine. The place surrounded and fell in on me like quicksand. I wasn't scared, though. I could breathe in this. I had accepted this world, the inhospitable one that projected shame and death on a backdrop of breathless beauty. It was, indeed, home.

I used a shovel to dig a hole. I'd remembered one this time. When it was deep enough, I poured the dirt from Jesse's grave into it. It had a different color and texture from the desert dirt. That was good. Perhaps he was part of it. I covered his dirt with some of the desert's and topped the whole with small stones. He said to bury him out here. This was the best I could do.

I stood out there as alone as a human being can be and eyed the emptiness in every direction. I willed her to show herself. I screamed her name. "Come here and join another bathed in someone else's blood who can't forget." Who knew? There may have been an army of us out there, men and women singed with the blood from boys whose brains the world and people in it had blown away, an army of us wandering the desert in dazed wonderment. I sat and listened to the silence. I waited.

XIV

My mother died a few years ago—iron to the end. When her cancer had progressed past the point she would tolerate, she arranged her death. The family physician administered a lethal dose of morphine and she slipped away. Becca and I held her hands, each weeping and whispering that we loved her. She smiled at that, but did not say it in return. Once she died, Becca and I wept in each other's arms until Becca lifted her head from my shoulder, wiped the tears from my face and said, "A rip-snortin' bitch to the bitter end." We both almost choked with laughter. The doctor was appalled.

Her funeral could not help but recall my father's. His was a life blotted out too soon by too many regrets. She had lived long and she had lived the life she pleased. Her death did not kindle in me the need to reorder the world. Her death was peaceful. It just… happened. I had a greater intimacy with death than most by then. Death and I were comradely. When they lowered my mother's body into the ground, I thought of Jesse, and wondered if the pile of stones I had laid years before still marked the place where I tried to keep my promise to him.

Becca stayed a while after the funeral. She was (and still is) on her third and seemingly final husband, a Belgian with whom she's gained the confidence and grace to age. We got to catch up. One day, my leg was particularly bothersome; I guess I was limping quite noticeably.

"You never talk about that," she said.

"Why would I? Nothing to be done."

"Not the leg. The whole thing."

She waited to see if I'd walk through the door she'd opened, but I did not.

"I imagine if something like that happened to me," she said, attempting to make light, "I'd be alluding to it every ten minutes, trying to make myself seem romantic and dangerous."

"I was dangerous all right."

"None of that was your fault," she said soothingly.

"Yes it was," I replied with a matter-of-fact smile, touching her hand to tell her it was okay.

She knew better than to argue and she probably knew I was right.

"You were trying to do a good thing," she added. "You tried to show him some kindness."

Though I was long past trafficking in my own innocence, I hadn't seen it that way. I still thought about Jesse, and often wondered if I could have helped him had I been… better. To this day, I close my eyes and hear the blast and see the blood spray appear on the police car window like a trick of animation; I see the gun barrel jump to his head, feel his blood's warmth sting my skin.

I shake it off.

Becca was looking at me as if she read my thoughts, with one of those oh-so-sympathetic faces that reminded me.

"Do you remember what you said to me at graduation?" I asked her.

She looked puzzled and then her face lit up.

"Yes!" she exclaimed. "I do. I actually practiced it in the cab on the way over. I felt so guilty that I wasn't going to stay. I think I wanted to be a living, breathing greeting card and leave you with some pearl of wisdom to tide you through. You were all alone." She laughed heartily at herself. "I said, '*you've got wings, brother. Fly!*'" and I probably made some wing-like gesture. So ridiculous, but I felt so guilty."

I started laughing. The words that had launched my grand crusade might as well have spilled from a fortune cookie.

"Those words changed my life," I told her, still smiling.

"They were true. You knew it."

I let that sink in.

"I crash landed."

"The price," she replied. "You probably knew that, too."

"I really went out there looking for something, you know?"

"What?"

"A sense of place," I supposed, thinking aloud. "Maybe home."

"It seems you found it."

"It found me," I told her. "It's like the place took me, bathed me in blood, turned me into something else that could live within it. Then it spat me to the ground and supplied this place here, where I could bury myself deep enough to keep warm." I looked at her. She seemed to understand.

"I guess that's home," I said.

She and I talked more those few days than we had in our entire lives. It had taken that long for me to get to know my sister, and for her to know me. She overcame her terror of horses and learned to tolerate jazz. I, in turn, became less reflexively contemptuous of fashion.

One night I played her an extraordinary song—one that consistently rips ground from beneath my feet to leave me stunned—overcoming my fear that she wouldn't find it as breathlessly moving as I did, and finally not caring. It starts as an anecdote of a man to whom fate has been typically indifferent; it ends as a psalm.

I saw Willie Mays
At a Scottsdale Home Depot,
Looking at garage door springs
At the far end of the fourteenth row.
His wife stood there beside him
She was quiet and they both were proud,
I gave them room but was close enough
That I heard him when he said out loud:

This was my country,
This was my song,
Somewhere in the middle there
Though it started badly and it's ending wrong.

This was my country,
This frightful and this angry land,
But it's my right if the worst of it might
Still somehow make me a better man.

The sun is unforgiving
And there's nobody would choose this town,
But we've squandered so much of our good will
That there's nowhere else will have us now.
We push in line at the picture show
For cool air and the chance to see
A vision of ourselves portrayed
As younger and braver and humble and free.

But that was him, I'm almost sure—
The greatest centerfielder of all-time
Stooped by the burden of endless dreams
—His and yours and mine.

This was my country,
This was my song,
Somewhere in the middle there
Though it started badly and it's ending wrong.
This was God's country,
This frightful and this angry land,
But if it's His will the worst of it might
Still somehow make me a better man.

* * *

Happenings twenty and thirty years ago affect me still, but I have made peace with them. I shelter my horses and watch as they're born. Happily, they are long-lived and I've only had to bury two. Not so lucky with the dogs and the cats. There's a well-stocked cemetery on my grounds.

I have some friends now, and I see Louisa once or twice a year. I taught her son to ride and now he comes to see me. I may one day teach his son. I went to Cindy's wedding.

I never married. Too wounded for that, I guess, or never met anyone appropriately and sufficiently damaged. Haven't tried very hard either. For some reason, I want to face this world alone. It seems proper to me. I cling to its more elemental things, its ground and ground creatures—the ones free from dreams of flight and eminence.

Each year I travel to the desert and sit at the place where Jesse died, where I laid stones to mark his place. I think of him and wish him peace in his idea of heaven. I get purposefully lost on old back roads, awaiting a woman in a brightly lit trailer, dancing and mourning her dead, like me, at home in this land of ghastly innocents.

THE END

About the Author

Photo credit:

Raised in New Orleans; Washington, D.C.; Germany; Missouri; Maryland; and elsewhere, Leonce Gaiter is the quintessential army brat—rootless, restive, and disagreeable. He began writing in grade school and continued the habit through his graduation from Harvard College.

His nonfiction writing has appeared in the *New York Times*, *New York Times Magazine*, *Los Angeles Times*, *The Washington Times*, *LA Weekly*, *NY Newsday*, *The Washington Post*, Huffington Post, Salon, and in national syndication. His noir thriller, *Bourbon Street*, was published by Carroll & Graf in 2005. His historical novel, *I Dreamt I Was in Heaven*, was published in 2011. He currently lives in Northern California.